RAGE AND PASSION

Lyrical Prose

JEAN-YVES VINCENT SOLINGA

FIRST EDITION

Little Red Tree Publishing, LLC,
635 Ocean Avenue, New London, CT 06320

Previous works published with Little Red Tree Publishing:

Clair-Obscur of the Soul (2008)
Clair-obscur de l'âme [in French] (2008)
In the Shade of a Flower (2009)
Landscape of Envies (2010)
Words Made of Silk (2011)
Impressions of Reality (2013)
Artist in a Pixelated World (2014)
Asymptotes at the Infinity of Passion:
The Untouchable Quest of Poetry (2015)
Created Realities (2017)
Paris: Genesis of a Muse (2019)

BOOK COVER
Prometheus joining the cause of happiness:
Stealing "Fire" for humanity.
Like a spy
—convinced of the nobility of his deed—
refusing to talk.
Prometheus is at the rare, quasi-romantic
intersection,
where few super heroes live:
A sentient awareness of fatalism.

From, "Of Titans, Supermen and Humanistic Heroes": In *Rage and Passion*. And the rational for the choice of this particular book cover: The Paul Manship's vision of a quasi-fragile figure for this Titan; not the physically dominating form of other representations. And, of course, the critical status of Prometheus' allegiance in two distinct worlds.

Layout and Cover Design: Michael Linnard, MCSD
Text in Forum, Times New Roman, Trajan Pro and Ariel.

First Edition, 2020, manufactured in USA
1 2 3 4 5 6 7 8 9 10 LSI 25 24 23 22 21 20

All photographs by kind permission of Jean-Yves Solinga.
Pages: iv, 93, and 131.

Front cover photo of the statue of Prometheus by the American sculptor Paul Manship, stands outside the Rockefeller Center in New York. This photograph is in the public domain.

Library of Congress Cataloging-in-Publication Data

Solinga, Jean-Yves
 Rage and Passion / Jean-Yves Solinga. -- 1st ed.
    p. cm.
 Includes glossary and index.
 ISBN 978-1-935656-63-0 (pbk. : alk. paper)
 I. Title.
 PS3612.A58565S77 2020
 811'.6--dc23

Little Red Tree Publishing LLC
635 Ocean Avenue,
New London Connecticut 06320
www.littleredtree.com

CONTENTS

FOREWORD

It is a rare occurrence indeed when a publisher begins to write a foreword to the Eleventh book, not least full-length book of poetry, from the same author. Such is the case with Jean-Yves Solinga's book, *Rage and Passion*.

The cover and title of any book, more so with a book of poetry, often brings together aspects of an author's collective thought processes, concepts and perceptions into close proximity and focus, in a visual form. What might seem to be disparate, mutually exclusive entities and concepts to the casual observer are in the mind of Jean-Yves brought together to stand logically together and in harmony. This particular cover image is of a statue of the Greek God Prometheus, by American sculptor Paul Manship, who gifted life to humanity from clay, then immeasurable enhanced this by the stolen gift from Zeus of "fire." Of the many 2D and 3D representations of Prometheus, Jean-Yves selected this modern interpretation of a young man, as could be seen anywhere today: Eschewing the highly muscle-bound dominating male figure often used.

It is interesting from the view point of an existentialist that the Greeks, most famously and in the absence of the christian God, conveniently and necessarily constructed a panoply of celestial characters to explain the absurdities of existence and humanity. Prometheus, was responsible for creation itself and the innate human trait of seeking knowledge, exploring, and continuous growth through his special act of benevolence on the one hand and the thief of its most unique qualities... without which maybe this book would not exist! Whilst there are obvious flaws in this explanation, I, like Jean-Yves find myself fatally attracted to the romance... maybe we would all have applauded Hercules as he freed Prometheus from his torment.

In Jean-Yves' first book Clair-Obscur of the Soul (2008) I wrote in the foreword that I had enthusiastically accepted his first manuscript for publication, "...because of its intensity, lyricism and insight into the essence of what it is to be human, in fact beyond and through to the heart and soul." The writing and publishing of ten books, to arrive at this point, has not diminished my thought about Jean-Yves. I have always wondered why he has not been more widely recognized as the poet of high quality, working assiduously at his art to reach even further into the soul of what it is to live in this world.

I once described Jean-Yves, in another foreword, as a "fearless," and I can think of no other fitting epithet more becoming a poet who is constantly reaching and searching for new ways to express his thoughts. Thankfully in that regard we are all the wiser, and knowledgeable, while being sublimely entertained.

Michael Linnard
New London, CT. 2020

Acknowledgement

To the memory of my father, Marcel Laurent Solinga, my mother Anna Félicie (née Ciccariello). And the memory of my brother Pierre Paul.

I want to recognize my sister Marie Louise Menders (who diligently found the picture from our living room, in Salé, Morocco); my son Robert Marcel, his wife Elisabeth and son Luc. My daughter Nicole Anne, her husband Marc Stasi, and their daughters Noelle and Luciana.

And especially, my wife Elaine, who has endured hours of my thinking and always been unfailingly supportive of my typing.

Jean-Yves Vincent Solinga
Gales Ferry, Connecticut 2020

PREFACE

This book continues my wanderings between two poles, two concepts, two of my short-cut views of life and living: The fragile, ephemeral weight of a human thought and the enormity *of the stuff* of the universe.

This duality of interest kept derailing the *tone* of my doctoral thesis. To paraphrase a constructive comment on one of my earlier drafts: "Jean-Yves, you are not writing poetry." For I had been looking, [particularly, at that time] mostly in French texts and writers, for analyses of human reflection on the Maghreban landscape of my youth.

Human intellect finding pieces of itself in the universe and yet, still feeling alone, is not new; but I was not sure how to approach it academically. And then, I found "my calling," on that winter's night, driving back, from graduate studies at the University, at Storrs, when a little beach (Sidi Moussa), spoke with its hot breath on the nape of my neck. A sort of dialog, with the "desert-shepherd"—the Moses [Lord Sidi Moussa, in Arabic]—and the narrator/writer, of my poetry. Thus, my writing, began to take form. It became the driving/guiding energy, for the genesis of my work.

The North-African landscape of my youth, would indirectly allow, for both, research-study, as well as, rich lyricism: As exemplified and described in the segment of the very first paragraph of *Noces* (epigraph) by Albert Camus. For, I was struck by Camus' easy combination of crystalline, succinct thought, and yet, the fine lace of his poetic sentences: Seamlessly blended into the historic, cultural, and humanistic. Simply. Describing moments. Glances!

My book, is nevertheless inhabited by biblical figures, even if in a nihilistic, non-traditionally religious world.

The biblical figure of Moses, who took me back to the little beach of the Maghreb, and in the wake of which exist my early writings, returns in this book: Taking the narrator back to Marseille, to my American rites of passage, to my Army draft, deaths and assortments of emotions... all fertile places... *all very and safely fictionalized.*

I started with the concept that humans seem to have been "endowed" with the improbable luck of having evolved the ability, *to reflect on their own reflections.*

And I adapted, and often use, the tool of lyricism, to reflect on these moments. Using, for instance, the artistic drive, powered by creativity, as a practical antidote to the absurdity of life: Lyricism has a way of making the absurd... calculable.

So that, for instance, see an intellectually, "happy" Monet... dying, while looking at one his garden scenes.

Some of the poems in this book, take note of one of humanity's real pride: Its arrogance (even if, doomed) of superiority over the dumb/blind cosmos. [i.e. "Dying glance"]

Some of this was prompted by my viewing amazing, university-level YouTube programs, of cutting-edge topics of cosmology and physics: Isn't it just "so human," but to impose our control over the universe, by writing equations about it?

Poets do the same by writing poetry.

Nothing more controlling, than using the measure of the speed of light, encapsulating it in an equation, in an attempt to enlighten us! As though, the speed gives it gravitas. To then, be told that it does after curves, just about takes corners around big masses... it is particles... it is waves... it goes untold distances apparently through nothing. But.. now we think that the universe might (after all) be filled with "stuff" [black matter]. Got it?

While, all the while, our unassuming artist, seems to have been better equipped *to fully join the camps of poetry AND solidity.* The two poles, previously mentioned. This is on display in one of my poems' setting, where the narrator, is confronted on such convoluted and expansive things as "a lecture on the beginning of time," or some similar issue... and the reader's focus is turned to the microcosm of a co-ed sitting, a few feet from the narrator!

Or a lyrical daydream, with post-carnal visions, worthy of a Caravaggio canvas, that turns the reader's attention to earthy happiness. And yet, the narrator/protagonist, still mentions this vaporous glance.

After all, isn't this sensual presence next, to him, on the lumpy bed in Paris, not as much a reality of the cosmos?

Since my first readings of Albert Camus' and that first page of *Noces à Tipasa*, I had, specifically, found the comfortable, human, organic-rich, dirt as a metaphor for the eternal, yet fragile human happiness: Anchored in the eternal solidity of the *stardust-substance*... that is, the Mediterranean shoreline.

I am profoundly at peace there. Even during the howling February winter snowstorms, of my hours of writing about it.

Even with the inevitable *decrepitude* predicted by time, and my difficult return to see and smell "le Vieux Port de Marseille" of my parents... I, nevertheless, want nothing to do with the frigidity of some philosophies that, sometimes speak, in bitter terms, of *human* truths found in the bitter human condition. Or yet, its opposite: The bromide of escapism.

I am, rather, in Docteur Rieux, Sisyphus and Prometheus' camps: Fighting the gods and their laws!

I like to sprinkle *living* on the dirt of realism, as best as possible. Not unlike Camus, proposing to his reader, to consider Sisyphus *happy*, as he rolls his boulder under the *generous* sun.

Or, for instance, recalling my parents' tales of Oncle Jules, who, at the height of misery, of an occupied France, and during the added tactical mistake of an errant American bombing-raid over French civilians, ran back to the house, down the street, in order to retrieve the straw-wrapped wine bottle. He made it back safely; but I put this touching human trait on the same level as our unknown ancestor who went to the back of his cave to spread colored mud [probably feces-incrusted] to glorify, to this day, the wild game that gave food.

And with the swipe of a muddy hand did something that artists do every day: Stop time [and that kiss] ... in the space of time.

Life is not strictly organized. Nor is my life: Source of my poetry. Or that of the reader. Therefore, neither are the poems in this book. There is some grouping: Such as, around the "Tour Hassan," which brought (back)—to the front—biographical issues of the "Other." Indeed, some of my scribbled notes (now on my phone's notes-screen), instigated by an errant Proustian-thought, have given the visceral tone sought by poets: "Recovered memory," through tiny, black and white photographs, dating to my youth in Salé, Morocco. They prompted me to face the dilemma of my approach to the Maghreban landscape as purely aesthetic. And not ethnic/political/historic.

The poem on "La Tour Hassan" [the unfinished Minaret of what would have been a gigantic Mosque] came back into my present life. And I had to make emotional and logical space for her. "Imprinted beauty" is my ode to this setting that I have unreservedly loved, since playing on my bike.

Although at ease in my nihilistic corner of the universe, I have, like other writers, used the wealth of religions and various beliefs, codes, commandments, and restrictions to my advantage. Some of the best literature has evolved from violations of the norms.

Docteur Rieux, in Camus' *la Peste*, exists in a parallel universe: That of his own *secular bible*. Not unlike, in one of my previous poems, I contemplate a *rebellious prophet Abraham*, who without hesitation, challenges the divine command to kill his own son: Putting his son's welfare above the wishes of his God. Hence, he could have changed the genesis of a whole trace of Western, human, religious thought. It is, indeed, much harder, dangerous and weightier, to be rebellious like Sisyphus or Prometheus.

I write fiction. Or rather, in tone and purpose, I write *applied fiction*: Therefore, not unlike the way we prepare a student with the precepts of analyzing and looking at the world with arithmetic or advanced mathematics, but without going over every possibility. You give the student a ruler and tell him: "Now, go measure something!"

There is a topic, in this book, which required an adjustment in the fictionalization of reality: Real life events to be treated with consideration on their projection into the present. It inserted itself during my Doctoral thesis. It is still actual: My French identity in the Maghreban world. To which I answer in a non-verbal and symbolic way, with the precious picture of me, with Barka in her djellaba: I did not write a geo-political treatise... a little boy's tearful wave settled that argument years ago.

The experience of living, and the observation of human behavior, give the artist enough material to extrapolate. The addition of flexibility of language, the shades of paint etc.... are a matter of choice and particular talent and interest of the artist. A budding writer of great tales, in High School today, is going to use the same words as those used by Shakespeare but for his own purpose. In theory, all the necessary material is available.

Non-fiction [i.e. "real" reality] writing demands scrupulous research. Although, history-based melodramas, allow for reconstructive fillers. (with some raising of eyebrows: "Did the Queen really say that to her husband?") But for my part, in the mannerism of Proust, I like the flexible safety of the "pastiche": Where the artist can combine personalities or modify them at will. So that, even in a poem based on war-time, recalled or retold to me, I have always, changed major details or leap-frogged between events.

We have constructed gods: We surely can construct *realities*.

And, as I have written in previous introductions and prefaces, there is nothing more valuable to a writer's ears than: "She [it] sounds so real: Who is she?

I would like to recognize and thank Michael Linnard, of Little Red Tree Publishing, for his professional guidance and personal relationship through the years. He was there at the genesis of my first book.

Jean-Yves Solinga
Gales Ferry, CT (Summer of 2020)

Jean-Yves, at his favorite "thinking" spot. Painting (back left corner) of the Fountain of the Four Dolphins, in Aix-en-Provence, by Jeannette Olson. The Pont Neuf, in Paris, by Sugawara Suinji. The wine... a Bordeaux.

Au printemps, Tipasa est habitée par les dieux et les dieux parlent dans le soleil et l'odeur des absinthes, la mer cuirassée d'argent, le ciel bleu écru, les ruines couvertes de fleurs et la lumière à gros bouillons dans les amas de pierres. À certaines heures, la campagne est noire de soleil.

Albert Camus, *Noces*

In the Spring, Tipasa is inhabited by the gods and the gods speak through the sun and the smell of absinth, the silver coated sea, the raw-blue sky, the flower-covered ruins and the big bubbles of light in the rock formations. At certain times, the landscape is blackened by the sun.

Albert Camus, *Noces*

RAGE AND PASSION

Rage and Passion

"L'homme est la seule créature qui refuse d'être ce qu'elle est."
"Man is the only creature who refuses to be what he is."

"À ceux qui désespèrent de tout, ce ne sont pas les raisonnements qui peuvent rendre une foi, mais la seule passion… "
"To those who despair of everything, not reason but only passion can provide a faith." [note by j-y.s.: 'foi', 'faith' taken here as a philosophical, ethical belief]

Albert Camus, L'Homme Révolté. (1951)

Humankind… the putative winner of evolution.
Not the biggest or strongest.
More likely the smallest and luckiest.

In a universe of mostly hostile stardust and black matter,
it seems that compared to rocks…
on a planet made of rocks,
Earth is, indeed, some sort of paradise.

But upper sentient life
leads to troublesome self-reflection.

Instead of the apparent *satisfaction* of the African elephants
in the monotony of eons of rainy seasons,
our African ancestors, gave us instead,
humans
full of unrest and questioning.

———————————

One metaphor for human contentment,
Paradise,
seems to have started to feel more like a golden prison

———————————

The themes in our myths,
were based in human worries,
conceivable only by human minds:
Trying to make sense of their surroundings.

Myths…
gave some human reference to the inexplicable…
the scary, the unjust.

Story-telling:
Peopled by actors of a typical human spectrum of the *commedia*.

An intermingling of various forms
of arbitrary whims, from random gods.

Not unlike those, whom Albert Camus
accused of allowing "la mort des enfants."
The death of children.

And then the proverbial *apple* in a tree:
A stand-in for the "keys to the car."
Freedom from paternal judgement.

Dreamers and thinkers.
Members of the unsustainable heights of self-consciousness.
Repelled by the irreversible built-in contradictions of life.

Existence… non-existence.
Unacceptable pebbles in the shoe-ware of human condition.
That is:
Life in the shadow of its opposite.

And then,
the futility of any form of moral rebellion:
Trying to topple a non-existing ethical metric:
All, in the absence of any metric, from any divinity.

———————————

And yet!
It is in the very rebellious nature of human emotions,
that lies the glory of the effort.

Often child of the mundane,
it is often, indeed, full of nobility… *pride and prejudice.*

Human passion. Human **passions!**
Righteous: Because of their singularly human genesis.

Worthy… in an artist's eyes… of its pound of *eternity*.
There… on its museum wall.

As he sits, convinced, that
She will always remain at that coffee table.
Her glance, still smoldering.

A découpage outline of her body.
There on the bedroom curtains!

And…
in the midst of all this philosophizing
—and ironically as important—
the summer heat on the nape of his neck
and the mowing of the lawn.

The mowing of the lawn!
In order to please the neighbors' passing glance.

Life has its way of reestablishing its own priorities.

And now…this apparent solidity in the chest…
As though, mother-nature were refusing her nurturing,
by willfully withholding her once plentiful air…
her oxygen.

The anger! The rage!
The shrinking of everything.
Things. Time.
The sudden opaque flatness of the hospital walls.
The importance of the *miniscule-now:*
Versus the frustrating expanse of the outside world.

The once so peaceful
and exhilarating illusion of timelessness!

The disappearing next seconds.
The very temporal *fragility* of awareness.

Such as the vision of his mother's blue eyes,
by the World War One boy-soldier,
as his chest fills up with mud.

The newly-found, surprising inverse value
of the commonplace to its importance.

Upon returning from the jungle humidity of Viet Nam:
The *bolt of survivor-guilt,*
on the February-cold sands,
at the National Seashores on the Cape!

––––––––––––––––––

You hear, from *her* doppler-ganger:
A summon… for your attention, amidst the sweat-soaked sheets.

"You know that I can take things away."

"Your lungs will atrophy in a flow of black blood."
"And you will feel it all the way to whence you came…"

"… to nothing… to nothing."

And then… that *rage*… that *passion!*
Rage… rage, for having been given… the unwanted…
the unfair *knowledge* of finite time.

Fear of the next seconds abandoning you.
Leaving you. Leaving us.

And… only our passion and infinity… to reclaim them.

––––––––––––––––––

Let astrophysicists fill their boards with equations,
we know that they will lead to even more galaxies.
Universes within universes.
Cosmic matryoshka dolls!

While the artist and his mind, may have, all this time,
been using a vocabulary better suited to deal with the incomprehensible.

Extremes imbedded in time and space.

Humanity… itself… between the infinitely large or small.
The infinitely endless. Among multiple inert worlds.
Multiple curtains, hiding multiple wizards.

And all of it, just like for Dorothy, will turn out
just as prosaically disappointing.

Humans' quest and mythologies, meeting *those others*…
themselves products of their own clueless mythologies.

While, in their spare bedrooms,
artists surround themselves with reams of papers.
Having written fluvial Russian novels.
Now simply piled on top of grand-father' bureau.

Canvases, upon canvases!
Paintings: Full of *the furor of life.*

Passionate human answers,
found in the splendor of nature.
In the language of screaming oils.

In Arles,
an empty soul, singlehandedly battling the cosmos,
with *sunflowers* stacked behind a kitchen door.

Artists and poets, have, in their own way,
worked with the multidimensional calculus of metaphors.

Having lined up the alchemy of black pearls of musical notes:
giving *solidity* to whiffs of human freedoms
in the hearts of the *misérables* in the streets of Paris.

Sound of wood instrument incarnating the shyness of a fawn
in the underbrush… on a sleepy afternoon.

Chiseling striated marble:
to capture the smooth essence of youth in a winged cupid.

All of this drive, arguably starting with mud
on anonymous cavern walls:
To bring back what is no longer there.

This alternate world:
The world of artists and their art.

Manipulating, from their mind:
tenderness, depravities, jealousies.
As well as their antitheses.

The *agonies* of dying love.
Emotions that could fill the space of unbounded nebulae.
And yet *contained* in our mental pixels.

————————————

Nearly transparent paints:
Representing nearly transparent tears of religious ecstasies,
from untouched and untouchable Madonnas.

Slashes of flesh-crimson tint.
Engorged lips: made from orchid-petals,
echoing the unbridled lubricity of Courbet.

Plaintive repetitions of the heat of her *Iberian* surname
in a solo, from a murderous tenor:
Giving a face to treachery, on your drive home.

One more pass of the chisel, by a crazed Camille:
Accomplishing the artistic, religious equivalent of the "imposing of hands."

Turning mineral marble into flesh.
Rendering in stone, the crystalline reality of her throbbing heartbreak.

The amoral glorification and freedom.
The post-paradisiac, moral nudity of the couple.

The needed tabula rasa, advocated by the infamous *Marquis*,
from the restrains of religious morality… for the arts.

An amoral flight, with no Polar star:
Instead, just a self-guided system:
Advocated by latter *nihilist-moralists*.

The description of the luxuriant and luxurious sexual overlap
of the timidity of youth…
the aggressivity of a jaded lover:
In the same person…
in the same hour,
so haunting to the *poètes maudits*.

Poetic freedom, *transgressing poetically*
Einsteinian time-restrictions.

The rigid frigidity of the Heisenberg principle,
proving no match for the slippery mucus of human eroticism.

All and any other forms of the above,
trying to answer the quaint and tiresome questions
from physicists and cosmologists:
About time-travel and our *real place* in the universe.

Things like the laws of mass… of gigantic or minute matter.
Anti-matter… dark matter:
As though, all this would bring *her* back in your arms…
on that dance floor.

All living happily… in their own dimension…
in the humid folds of Human Passions.

So… while we can give a name to what powers our Sun,
we cannot ask *why **IT** should exist in the first place.*

Our poet, painter or musician, in their corner
have already internalized its warm rays
through a provençal olive grove.

Have already immortalized the moment.
In another *universe.*
A different dimension.

This huge inert star,
having been allowed to witness our lovers' summer kiss.

This dumb, lonely gaseous object,
given an honored place at the nuptials of mortal souls.

Spectacular solar presence:
no less than the giver-of-life for humanity.

Full of the primordial plasma.
Source of quasi-eternal energy and nuclear apocalypses.

Full of the earliest fascination for mankind:
This Sun-god:
Having been anthropomorphized,
consecrated as royal center of so much mythologies.

And yet,
with all that interaction with the creatures of this Earth.
All of this volume.
All of this omnipresence.
Incapable,
—for one second, in the eternity of things—
of *awareness* of the value of that kiss.

That afternoon… in the heat of the summer sun.

Of Greek mythologies and human envies

We get our mythologies from
sacred mounts, as well as writers, artists,
and the unappreciated Hollywood.

From gathering of thinkers and dreamers:
Unlikely descendants of their Greek predecessors.

Gifted constructors of landscapes of human envies.
Codifiers of iconic figures of our cultures.

Beings and events that arose
from essences of *human* fears.

From very normal questioning and longings.

Prompting humanity and humans,
to concoct age-old tales, sanctified by time:

Making the mundane, to make sense of strange things.

All of the above,
often… without re-inventing new *biblical* passages.

Re-creations on an alternate setting for life:
Made more believable, by our very yearnings to know.

To live, once more…
moments or alternative moments.

To live like… or unlike the protagonist:
Moments… of the reality of the impossible.

The spectacular… or the Other.

Absolutely free speculation.
Freedom upon freedom of speculations.

Fusion and fission of things:
as a gift
from the writer... the one... the *real creator.*

Words and worlds of limitless expansions.
Worlds of sciences fiction, invading worlds of realities.

Not unlike...
the unlikely existence of... *us.*
On this... the third rock from a minor star.
In our corner of a vague galaxy.

Because *these gods...* created by humanity
Do... at times... speak truthfully.

Arbitrary selection of moments of Hollywood's incarnations of our realities: Soylent Green,
The Planet of the apes, The Omega man: *the effects of runaway over-population, a pandemic and worldwide nuclear destruction.*

Of Titans, Supermen and Humanistic Heroes

Inspired by the scene, when Superman willingly gives up his powers for Lois.

Was it, Prometheus' nagging unease toward his status,
as a member of the Elysian group?

A built-in weakness, about his fidelity and allegiances:
giving him an appealing, quasi-human susceptibility,
and dangerous enemies?

Indeed, an unusual
touching trait for any demi-god.

Not fully in one camp.
And with powerful enemies.

This is a world beyond this one:
capable of inflicting… *eternal… immortal death.*

A non-ending condemnation:
a harrowing lesson for the inhabitants of mythology,

Prometheus joining the cause of *happiness:*
Stealing "Fire" for humanity.

Like a spy
—convinced of the nobility of his deed—
Refusing to talk.

Prometheus is at the rare, quasi-romantic intersection,
where few super heroes live:
A sentient awareness of fatalism.

And a willingness to act.

Prometheus, exemplifying a powerful, magnanimous
bodily sacrifice, for the good of others.

Nous sommes tous Docteur Rieux. *

Oran, Algérie (1947)

"Can one be a saint without God? That's the problem, in fact the only problem...."
The plague *Albert Camus*

To be civilized...
when everything else is not.

To believe...
when your side has lost:
and will always lose.

To pray...
when no-one is listening.

To lay down your bet... using your eternal life...
when the roulette-wheel is defective.

And still,
the secular *moralists* try to control, with their *bare* hands,
the silt of despair.

With...
no expectations, no illusions.

With none of...
the fanatical, delusional mortification
of flesh and soul, of the medieval luminaries:

Those convinced of their claim of celestial vestals.

But rather, just a simple man
facing the randomness of evil.

Ethical sainthood... does exist in non-existent support.
It is a lonely, ardent... red-hot confession,
made to a *deaf silhouette,*
behind a pudic wooden screen of a side-chapel confessional.

Secular sainthood is knowing... *knowing...*
that your anonymous brick... enriched by its very common origin ...
adds to the noble human integrity of the wall.

Humankind having all along constructed its own gods:
the *Righteous-Justes* among us, decided to build their own
from the scattered pieces.

Ones... with the cleared-eyed acceptance
of poetic fragility.

With all the darkness of personal doubts
and the organic, unctuous passions of *life and living.*

The relative strength of the adversaries in the struggle
was never in doubt.

The cosmos and things *can and will do as they wish.*
While the good Doctor
—losing his battle—
can look toward the Maghreb
and the late Mediterranean-crimson wetness of the sun.

*[We are all Doctor Rieux]

Erotic Supplications

A plaintive gentleness, characterized her protest.
Nature and the natural
had managed to keep the instinctive *drive of evolution* during all these eons.

The act… had been repeated in its prosaic ways:

But it was, upon a flashback
—among morning coffee fumes—
that the setting's, quasi-religious imagery, was revealed.

A bed… more like an altar…
gave this supplicant's willing surrender
its cosmic dimension.

Whiffs of Comedy in a Tragic Storm

Based on a scene in Au revoir les enfants, *by Louis Malle, where the camera zooms in on a doomed Jewish youngster: he is hiding in a French religious school and is laughing at the antics of Charlie Chaplin* The Immigrant *on the screen.*

Crystalline nature of the purity of contrast:
Hilarity of the chaotic, uncontrolled movements of the *Tramp*.

Temporary split in the tragic layers of the setting:
Adding to a nagging guilt for the viewer.

This… a visceral… instinctive laughter
in the midst of impending death.

The whole Drama,
impose—as if off stage—on the viewer and his soul.

An aura of quasi-divine, fore-knowledge and submission
as to the fate of these miserable students.

The helplessness of the audience
as a stand-in for an impotent Greek chorus.

Unbearable dichotomy of laughter in the middle of horrors.
Life and living, contain too many examples of these extremes:

Reminiscence of the plaintive echoes
of violins played by Shoah prisoners.

Chiaroscuro of extremes,
worthy of the bloodier shades of a Caravaggio.

Producing in us, a rictus made of exhaling gulps of laughter:
Akin to sickly hiccups.

"… like adding, salt on sugar cantaloupe slices: Giving intensity to sweetness because it alternates… taking momentarily the enjoyment away… thus, our not taking the sweetness for granted." [from author's notebook, about his first reaction to re-reading of this finished poem]

Of Phaedra and the Minotaur

Camus felt more at ease in the grittiness of Greek mythology than Christianity.

The Minotaur:
the offspring from a bored housewife and a pure-white bull.

Phaedra:
Susceptible to incestuous, emotional lust:
A women's self-destructive passion, for her step-son.

Grecian mythology,
with earthy, scandalous themes.

Sundrenched world:
With a stage of incomparable white-marble columns,
with filigreed designs.

Peristyles:
Overlooking the resting places of classic battles,
reaching, with geometric precision,
into a sea of deep-blue skies.

Echoed below,
by the gentle Mediterranean:
Eternally kissing, without harm, its rocky shore.

This is the solar world, where ancient moralists
had conceived classical signs of guiding truths.

Truths… found after all this time,
like sparkling pieces of priceless floor-mosaic,
left behind by wise men.

A setting full of a humanity
with its *unvarnished*
complexities and obsessions…
deeply sinful ways…
and verbal oratory.

A world such, as a conflicted man-beast!
A pathetic, former great royal soul rendered by *love*,
Disheveled and half-clothed,
on the striated blue marble.

A world and humanity,
unchanged since its early days.

With no preaching, no esoteric religious canons
and dogmatic commandments.
But rather the simple and immediate presences
Of things good… evil.

And the intervening, extreme choices:
Leading to each.

Vestal and Flesh

He remembered having always seen *her* as
quasi-vestal…
behind her professor's desk.

An incorrigible romantic,
he had risked his fortune, on her personal and professional guidance:
In his quest, in the torrid swirls of literary fictions.

The centuries, languages or settings, did not matter:
He would always naturally transpose the action onto himself.

In class, her voice
would concretize the textual passions from the page:
With a quasi *organic* vocalization of certain passages.

Such that, after months of pursuing various dashing heroes,
and long-haired heroines,
he had reconstructed, in his soul,
all matter of secretive rendezvous
for their intimacies.

All of these virtual emotions, had traversed to the other side of solidity:
Becoming quite real for him.

Telling her, one day,
in a perceptive, if intellectual way:
"Like Flaubert, I cannot keep my worlds of Romanticism and Reality separate."

"I exist and suffer in both."

In his young soul,
this confidence was a complete declaration of his love.

She kept her renowned perfect composure.

IT never happened again:
Never daring to determine if he had touched her.

… years later… at a symposium,
she reappeared in his life.

To his stupefaction, her mere presence,
now surrounded by her new supplicants,
rekindled, in an instant,
every sparks of jealousy found in every crevasse of texts
he had ever read.

She had aged miraculously:
The way vestals should:

In the protected fiction, of untouched, and untouchable perfection.

———————————————

The rest is magic-dust…

… finding himself, opposite to her, in a dimly-lit bedroom.
The silence is painful.
She looks radiantly appetizing, for a deity.

No woman, in his past, had ever had
her sinuously pulsating aura.

A trace of a smile.
A beatitude, bordering on the impossible:
The sensually-telepathic.

Who? What? Had brought her back?
Intact?

Across from her,
he was petrified against his wall.

Will she remain lubricious in his arms,
for their first time?

Will she still smell of perfumes from Grasse,
as in the hallways of yesterday?
Will she have a special vocabulary reserved for him

in the nuptial shadows?
Will she have that throaty carnality of fallen angels,
when aroused?

Will she start getting dressed,
as his whole body is still craving?

Will he associate her
with that particular flinty smell of sweaty exhaustion?

All the while,
seeing temple-fumes from smoldering incense,
placed on her taut stomach muscles.

An alternate reconstruction of Gustave Flaubert's "L'Éducation Sentimentale" with a carnal consummation of the relationship between Frédéric and Madame Arnoux.

Vestale et Charnelle

Il se souvenait l'avoir toujours vue…
quasi-vestale…
derrière son bureau de professeur.

Un incorrigible romantique.

Il avait risqué sa chance d'être
personnellement et professionnellement guidé par elle, durant sa quête,
à travers les tourments torrides des fictions littéraires.

Les siècles, les langues, ou les milieux ne comptaient pas:
Il transposait naturellement l'action sur lui-même.

En classe… sa voix…
concrétisait les passions textuelles de la page :
avec une vocalisation *organique* de certains passages.

De telle façon, qu'après des mois de poursuites d'audacieux héros,
et de héroïnes aux longs-cheveux :
il avait reconstruit, en son âme,
toutes sortes d'endroits secrets, pour *leurs* moments d'intimité.

Toutes ces émotions virtuelles, avaient évolué de l'autre côté de la solidité
quotidienne :
devenant, pour lui, pratiquement réelles.

Lui faisant déclarer un jour,
d'une manière perceptive, si quand même intellectuelle :
« Comme Flaubert, je ne peux pas garder séparés mes univers
Romantiques et Réalistes.

« J'existe et souffre dans les deux.»

Pour une jeune âme… *cet aveu*…
était son entière déclaration d'amour.

Elle maintint sa fameuse impassibilité.

CELA… ne se répéta jamais :
N'ayant jamais eu le courage de savoir si elle en avait été touchée.

… des années plus tard… à une conférence…
Elle *réapparut* dans sa vie.

Stupéfié… par sa présence-même :
alors entourée de ses nouveaux soupirants,
elle éveilla, instantanément,
tous les tisons attiédis de jalousie
que l'on trouve dans toutes les crevasses des textes,
qu'il avait lus.

Elle avait vieilli miraculeusement :
comme doivent le faire les vestales.

Protégées dans la fiction.
Intacte et intouchable.
Parfaite.

Le reste… est fait de poudre magique…
…
… se trouvant, face à elle, dans la pénombre d'une chambre :

Un silence qui fait presque mal.
Elle est radieuse à croquer… pour une divinité.

Aucune autre femme de son passé n'avait jamais eu
cette aura sinueuse et palpitante.

Un soupçon de sourire.
Une béatitude : à la limite de l'impossible.
Sensuelle. Télépathique.

Quoi ? Qui… l'avait-elle ramenée à lui?
Intacte ?

Face à elle :

il était pétrifié contre son mur.

Restera-t-elle lubrique dans ses bras :
pour leur première fois ?

Gardera-t-elle ses parfums de Grasse,
comme dans les couloirs d'hier ?

Aura-t-elle un vocabulaire particulier,
réservé pour lui…
pour les ombres nuptiales ?

Aura-t-elle cette voix rouée charnelle des anges déchus :
lors de leur éveil sexuel ?

Commencera-t-elle à se ré-habiller
alors qu'il la désirera encore de tout son corps?

L'associera-t-il à ces relents de silex de l'exhaustion remplie de sueur ?

Alors que, du temple,
il observera des nuages de fumée de l'encens brûlant :
placé sur son ventre plat… musclé.

Une reconstruction alternative de « l'Éducation sentimentale » de Gustave Flaubert, avec la consommation charnelle du rapport entre Frédéric et Madame Arnoux.

Saint Sulplice Seminary

To a background of memories from a college "year-abroad": Paris, late 1960's

Dorm-life, for them, had been:
"Like boot-camp for intellectuals."

The proverbially-paired odd couple
of university housing machinery.

Making for inseparable friendship.
Different backgrounds and philosophies.

Challenging diversity:
Leading to late-night bull-sessions

Every conceivable and unconceivable topics.
None of them taboo.

Disagreeing with intellectual panache, on everything.

———————————

"You called me! … of all people?"
"Yes… I needed to share this with you."

———————————

Having drifted apart after graduation,
one of the them: Now a future seminarist,
wanted to personally share his decision with his nihilistic,
ex-debate opponent.

Finding his roommate's secular ethics:
"Of an empty universe…"
"full of the nobility of human morality."

"I will bring it with me in my seminary studies.
I wanted to let you know."

Two expatriates, ex-warriors of the 1970's Paris, having their commemorative Alsatian beer.

University Studies in France

Sciences Po (Paris '68)

The miracle was…
that they had been in a Truffaut movie
without noticing it…

… so seamless and complimentary,
had the evolution of all their relationships been.

Things and people appeared and dissolved at café tables:
Fancifully,
as though attracted by the clouds of acrid European Tabaco.

Leaving deep stigmata on his soul.

Thus…
making the improbable look… retrospectively….
Privileged.

As though, ordained
by secular, mischievous, lubricious gods.

It was not until… on the return plane,
that all the links… felt like scenes.

Unbreakable and unavoidable sequences
presented themselves.

Various locations
Could literally trigger levels of discourse:
An historic event. An iconic statue:
Les Misérables, le Baiser.

And at times… trivial events would end… the next morning…
at someone's favorite pâtisserie.

Revealing, in the process, the frightful fragility
of bits of happiness in all our lives.

The haphazard, ephemeral nature of relationships
and their future Proustian memories.

There seemed to be no illogical filming-continuity.
As though the city had its own immutable laws:
A cosmic poetic license from the clock.

The gentle societal relativism:
the freedom of "Au naturel" instead of the anatomical "naked."

And quoting some convenient philosophy,
as a basis for defense.

The quasi-biblical genesis of their acquaintance,
started with the typical nonchalance about rules of
"faire la queue at Sciences Po?"

And the very telling answer
"None."

Added, to her emotional counter-currents:
Her femininity and yet, her virility.

An iron-will, combined with a bird-like febrility.

Absolute self-direction:
And yet…an open-ended, non-judgmental disponibility.

Perfect inhabitant for the social revolutions of the moment:
Soul and body.
Body and soul.

Cinematography of unrolling:
unscripted hours, in miniscule rooms.

Nuit américaine-shadows in a late-summer day:

Notre Dame, laced-designs:
silhouetted in crimson.

Coming home from Paris, having… apparently, lived in a Truffaut movie.

Translucence

Irony… the heartbreaking irony!
The boring, unstoppable imposition of finality on things,
producing an opposite reaction:
She…
kept, instead, reappearing in the vaporous silence of his morning coffee:
Apparently more solid now…
for having vanquished the grayish dullness of space and time.

Her glance…
full of the rich agnostic darkness of black-holes.
—not weakened by the phantasmagoric voyage to this part of his present.

Could this explain the ethereal, bottomless energy,
found in otherwise decrepit artists?

Their contemplation upon their own imminent oblivion,
somehow condensing… their *thought.*

Pure thought!
Disincarnated entity. Free of cosmological rules.
Thought… whose limits are made of the elasticity found in human
imagination.

Reality reduced in the broth of stellar dust,
by evaporating the grit of the secular:

The most cherished memories,
thus, protected for our present.

… *She…* was everywhere:
In the masculine stylish intonation of a passing woman.
Street scene full of the same aggressive sexual ambivalence:
"La beauté du diable"…
In the purified words from his catechism days.

And suddenly... ex machina... this simple two-note violin prelude:
As though produced by the running of the bow on taunt stomach muscles.
Not unlike an inventive... knowing... foreplay.

His *quieter* days, now constantly re-inventing *madeleines* from his past.
But it was the dignity of the unforced nature of this past:
Invading the otherwise reserved, reptilian part of his brain:
Searching into the remnants of sticky, organic happiness...
Where the earthy nourishment of art exists.

... And yet...
"All these academic degrees! All this manmade weaponry!" he sighed,
And the heart persists in taking refuge in the maternal.
The deeply gratuitous and forgiving.

And why not?
These moments... were his claims on *His* past:
Giving the artist an assured arrogance among mortals.

He would replay the scenario:
An entrance into a faculty meeting:

She... on the opposite far wall.
No verbalization. Just oblique glances...
*and **they** were reliving intimacies!*

"No M.I.T. machine has yet been able to replicate this!"
He would express at the lunch table:
In a non-sequitur that would confound his listeners:
Accompanied by furtive glances
toward the privileged slices of her peanut butter sandwich.
As he whispered the prayer of ex-lovers.

Closing his eyelids and fervently hoping
for one more favor from those silent gods:
"May they all be eternal romantics."

Still amazed by the ebullition of sensuality exhibited in older impressionists; and the very human frailties of the gods of Greek mythology.

Youth and the Grande dame

A fable

She had been the incarnation of decorum:
Impeccable desk. Hand-written thank-you notes:
With fore-telling sinuous lettering.

A constant awareness of echelon-status:
With unfailing recognition of ultimate distancing from the top.

Steely-blue eyes... behind steel-rimmed glasses:
The whole, packaged in a fortress-like private life.

Rumors of cold winds of interpersonal disinterest:
Proof of sensual and sexual dysfunctions.

All of the normal calumnious jealousies,
towards someone, personally and academically untouchable.

And then... a reassignment years later.

Now a colleague.

A regular invited-guest
to her physical and... emotional Sanctum Santorum.

And witnessing... a breathtakingly, incandescent world
of post-paradisiac, amoral freedom:
All, without a hint of redemptive guilt.

Unexpected visceral, unknown side, of a usually reserved "grande-dame" of the faculty senate.

The Real Death of Paradise

The ultimate world of invented answers:
Hollywood. The mythology factory.

At times, a surprisingly touching, human construction,

From mud on cave walls, to screen pixels of glitter:
They feel like pure extracts of concrete visions of our yearnings.

This maligned medium, can, at times,
viscerally captures the glorious arrogance of sentient life forms.

Somehow, this modern-day Ulysses, with his primordial cries,
this Hollywoodian schoolhouse pedagogy,
with its surgical message-packaging,
have a righteous, classical ascetism.

Just an ambiguous blasphemed name of *a divinity*.
Proper human discomfort zone,
for the enormities of an enormous universe.

Letting the sounds and presence of things
Speak for the unspeakable:
Hence *le Plaisir du texte* in its best multi-layered richness.

Giving back to nature… what nature knows best: Stellar nobility.

No need for fist pounding into the wet sand!
It is just and proper, that "man's dominion" …
then destruction… of this
—a multi-trillion chance gift to him—

Would end on this classical staging:
of pathetic anger…
useless tears…
and deserved loss

for whatever beauty
the world, unconsciously, gave to us.

Based on Charlton Heston's scene at the conclusion of the "Planet of the Apes."

The Last Elephant On Earth

Inspired by a program on an "Elephant orphanage" in central Africa

Redemption…
starts with in the quiet certitude of its first step.

In the appropriately lonely, oppressive heat
of a makeshift sanctuary.

Thorough the blasphemous symbolism of a chain-link fence.

And index extended to scratch the brow of a tiger.
A bowl of baby-food paste for an orphaned gorilla.

Individual souls, in the anonymity of mosquito bites,
re-creating a *garden* that never had been.

Mythologies and sacred book:
Appearing as smart encryptions.

And, rather…
not understood, as *future*-telling, magic mirrors.

Untold Years in the Future

A fable

The galactic war, would be lost for the left-over pieces
of the earthly-based descendants.

With no alternative,
but to issue a virtual white flag.

A cosmological enemy of humanity:
With unstoppable skills.

Their frigid technical, non-human minds,
Worlds-apart from earthlings.

No mental encryption could resist their attacks.
Human ways, and quaint habits would disappear.

Cold efficiency,
being the only tool for space survival.

Unbending, fanatic humanists,
on this ravaged third rock:
flying around with their illogical habits.

And… from among them, a commandant
full of his grainy, organic, terrestrial pride.

From among the ragged descendants,
Of these disheveled humanists
on this ravaged third rock
—the third rock, from a minor star—

straight out of their mythology:
A captain-Kirk type would emerge.

Who… in a desperate move,
with no permission,
no official code, no meetings,

would send, in a miniscule amount of data,
a challenging proof of undeniable superiority.

The rest of the story became folklore…
with reference to some obscure David and Goliath tale.
The earthlings had won peace!

The captain had utterly confused
and incapacitated the communications of the enemy.

A seemingly impregnable, lyrically-based language:
Baffling the most powerful, interpreting computers.

« Comme une pierre que l'on jette dans l'eau vive d'un ruisseau
Et qui laisse derrière elle des milliers de ronds dans l'eau
Comme un manège de lune avec ses chevaux d'étoiles
Comme un anneau de Saturne, un ballon de carnaval
Comme le chemin de ronde que font sans cesse les heures
Le voyage autour du monde d'un tournesol dans sa fleur
Tu fais tourner de ton nom tous les moulins de mon cœur. » *

"Round like a circle in a spiral, like a wheel within a wheel
Never ending or beginning on an ever spinning reel
Like a snowball down a mountain, or a carnival balloon
Like a carousel that's turning running rings around the moon
Like a clock whose hands are sweeping past the minutes of its face
And the world is like an apple whirling silently in space
Like the circles that you find in the windmills of your mind!

In the distant future… a war for life or death. For the survival of "what it is to be human." The desperate captain for the earthlings, wins peace by showing his side's unquestioned superiority: Sending a break-proof code in a language based on the lyricism of "les moulins de mon coeur."

* Lyrics and music by Michel Legrand: "Les moulins de mon coeur." See index

Army Tech

The *soldier* at his console, in complete, ergonomic comfort:
The screens,
showing various angles of Hell-on-earth.

Instantaneous vaporizing of bodies and lives:
Surgical elimination of ant-like movement.

Followed by eerily-pastoral, desert quiet.

Organic *things* neutralized.
Mission accomplished!

The dream of wars "well-waged,"
after lessons from the *Great War* of the trenches:

Mud and body parts,
co-mingled, with hours of soldiers' agony.

… innocent question…
of innocent side-conversation:
to fill awkward silence…
at family function.

"So… I understand you have this new, excellent technical position?"

"No longer… I had to retire and get counseling."

"The last few seconds on the screen were unbearably inhuman!"

Speculation on the future emotional damage from virtual military battles.

The Smartest… of the Savannah

Thought-poem: reflections on witnessing the primordial activities of an early member of our specie: Quasi-sort-of-animal, that would eventually evolve into mankind: The eventual inventor of mustard gas.

Not unlike the hypothetical,
the professorially-proposed ethical dilemma:

Being at the birth of a baby… *"Adolph Hitler."*

That is the ultimate image of this hirsute animal's future:
Helpless, in the dangerous setting of the African savannah.

Escaping death, three times a day.
Huddling together, in the cold rains of winter.

Females, barely able to birth their young.

Constantly, running away from predators:
Babies gripping their mother's hair.

Their evolving brains
Devoting full capacity for survival.

And then… this smelly mass of fur.
Our expressive… wide-eyed, pathetic grandparents,
will inherit it all.

The real kings of the jungle!
Masters of what they see!

They will even divert rivers.
Built magnificent arched aqueducts.

… and… arenas
to torture beasts, and their own.

Master… the dark sciences.
Engineer… the alchemy of Mustard gas.

A Night at the Theater of the Absurd

A nihilistic prophet Job

Pieces of her:
Desperately blowing on dying embers.
Gladly giving up the last vestiges of life from his lungs.

He needed to see her glance once more.
To dive again into her black-ink, feminine virility!

Her birdlike fragility, hiding behind a surprisingly dominant presence:
Dominatrix of all that had defined him.

Mistress of the various pieces of his unrepentant soul…
Now… simply laid out,
like a poor, Maghreban shepherd's possessions, on the desert floor.

He felt no shame of his *nudity* in front of her… his true deity.
An atheistic Job, with no believes to offer…
Instead… offering his ultimate gift…
his last precious human and sentient breath.

Sadly knowing… that all that would remain after him,
would be smells of cardboard scenery
in a theater filled by a willing audience:

Bravely… and still… waiting their turn… for Godot.

Une âme vertueuse

"La désintégration des standards d'humanité d'un monde civilisé, pendant les guerres, rend les vertueux d'autant plus précieux." [un autre commentaire, infusé de Cognac, venant de l'autre coin de la pièce]

Le Panier, Marseille (~1942)

La mère *célibataire* avait été proprement diffamée
par les matrones du deuxième étage:
« Une putain : c'est tout ce qu'elle est ! »

Elle a droit à plus de viande de cheval
pour ces coupons de rationnement!...
et elle veut que l'on s'occupe de sa fille! »

—————————————————

Une voix de la porte, au fond du couloir.
La femme froide, intellectuelle.
Celle qui utilise le *subjonctif.*
Une nonne *défroquée,* on dit.

"S'il y a une putain ici…
Elle est parmi vous.
Faites venir sa fille chez moi… n'importe quand…
Elle sera nourrie et hors de danger.

J'ai connu *votre* monde de religiosités…
Il me reste de ses carrés de sucre favoris! »

A Righteous Soul

"The disintegration of human standards in times of war, make the righteous among us, that much more precious." [more Cognac fueled comment from the corner of the room]

Le Panier, Marseille (~1942)

The "single" mother had been properly vilified
by the matrons of the third floor.
"A whore: That is all she is!"

"She gets more horsemeat
than allowed by her food stamps!...
and she wants one of us to take care of her daughter!"

––––––––––––––––––––––––

A voice from the doorway, at the end of the hall.
The cold, intellectual woman.
The one who uses the *subjunctive*.
A "defrocked" nun, they say.

"If there is a whore here…
it's among the rest of you.
Send her daughter to me… anytime…
she will be fed and safe!"

I've seen your world full of godly things…
I still have her favorite sugar cubes!"

Sleepy Morning Haze

Paris (circa Happiness)

In the unfathomably distant future of things,
We will have come full circle.
Looking around the post-apocalyptic, empty stage:
still waiting…
for Becket to identify his Godot.

Philosophers, writers and poets.
Painters and ex-lovers, will have told us so:
Yes… civilizations, will have evolved
from the granular-nothing.

To find our own reflection.
Or, maybe… another *intelligence* looking back.

An entity, just as passionate
and just as clueless as our own.

Adding to nothing.

————————————————

Not unlike Plato's Cave:
Most of us, will have been looking for its entrance.
To find the true realities in the sunlight.

Instead of looking at our objects of desire
among the shadows on the back wall.

In between, we will have been distracted
by the smart discoveries of cosmologists.

The frigid mechanics of the infinitesimal small and large.
Still guessing as to where and *why we are,*
and… to what end?

We will still have been playing notes of a symphony,
with firmly intricate cosmological rules.

But with an absent composer:

Debussy's *Nocturnes*
interpreted through bits of light and sound from analyzers!

Meanwhile… in the quaintness of recital-halls,
the musical score will have reproduced
sighs, sorrows and jealousies
that had meant so much.

Cosmologically precious:
Human—*invented*—Beauty.

Whispers, from sweaty, sanguine-lips,
heard…
then codified into lyricism.

Reconstructed in brushstrokes
onto museum walls.

All very human and ethereal things:
Ironically turning out as our best answer, in a universe
incapable of enjoyment.

———————————————

Back to my place… in this lumpy bed… next to her.

Early morning. Deux grands cafés-crème.
Place de Clichy. That glance! That glance!
and…
Tomorrows and Tomorrows…

Small College Town

Rarefied world of academia.
More often, textbook inverse of evolution:
Wherein, feline quickness, gives progeny.

Battlefields, found in oak-lined studies.
Or the circular sanctum of sycophants, nearest some podium:
Where crystalline truths, are hinted at, from brilliant minds.
Elegantly. Seamlessly.

Lectures: Like ones from prophets
—in some ancient temple—
where followers would refrain from looking directly at deities.

Here… the weapons
were chiseled constructions from eternal concepts.
With chevrons on caps and gowns,
worn as proudly as Romantic-era Hussars.

Reputations as unassailable as life tenures.
As fragile as next scandal.

————————————

He…
had been the incarnation of all and any of these pieces of his being:
As he leaned toward his colleague's wife lips.

Hearing… in his dissolving soul,
words heard all around:
"He shows such amazing purity and knowledge of various Ethics."

Inspired by the heartbreaking duality found in great personae of the art and academic worlds:
world class intuitive scientists and exquisitely sensitive musicians with horrid personal choices.

The Dogs of Chernobyl

It is within the dignity… in the ordinary,
that we recognize the nobility in the act.

From between her bony legs:
wisps of warm humidity announcing the birth.

She gently… instinctively…
turned her powerful jaws towards
the remaining… *only living* puppy.

Licked him clean
of the pieces of placenta.

She had viscerally contributed,
to return life to this infernal place.

*Inspired by a "Télématin" French news segment [circa January 2020] on the survival
of dogs around the radioactive debris, at Chernobyl.*

Spoils of War

Thoughts on the children of American G.I.'s, of post Viet Nam War.

Battles and killing:
Human nature at its most elementary.

The lunacy of the arbitrary,
like some Dada-esque cyclotron.

Elementary particles of humanity
stressed to their disintegration.
The killing, the bombing and the maiming…
and the instinctive.

The primal instinctive:
Of finding escape in a faceless, body-heat embrace.

The ironic survival of the flesh, from the paddy-fields,
transfigured through the available proximity of another flesh.

Temporary peace,
in the microcosm of a rented room:
Full of the flinty smell of diabolical links.

That of the vicious cycle of Faustian bargain:
One hour of quiet bliss… for a contemplated orphaned life.

This whole apocalyptical scene…
located on some nameless spot…
on some battle-field aerial-photographs…
at some headquarters.

Of Cultural Differences and Happy Endings. Nevertheless

He was part of some huge maneuver:
At a standstill in the red Georgia clay.

Late fall rains.
Wet… and appropriately home sick.

Wandering privates,
avoiding work-details:

Nervously slithering
away from bootcamp sergeants.

Military draftees:
Dutifully, volunteering for military things.

But then… cultural habits are second nature:
He volunteered for the kitchens.

———————————

"What are you doing in my kitchen?!"
"What did you do… private?"
"Nothing sergeant."

"I'll show you nothing!"
"You see these cages of onions… pick them,
one by one… and remove their loose skin!" …

…Interlude and confusion
due to the private's positive attitude and demeanor:
"Who sent you here… really?"
"I'm French. I like kitchens. I volunteered."

More confused silence:
"Private! How do make your white sauce?"
"You mean Béchamel?" …

A French immigrant in the U.S. Army. (Winter '68)

Newly off the boat

"I hope… that I did earn it."*

He had left his old skin on board:
Past train-station shoe-shines, hawkers of diners' menus,
Pan-handlers.

The exoticism of a racially, biforked, street-scene.

One thing in common…
He had it, probably… made!

He had one nose
Like the well-dressed…

One nose…
Like all the well-healed in this town.

The infliction of "two noses"
Seemed to be reserved to *those*…

The obvious Others.

He was safe in his anonymous-conformity:
All prepared to succeed in *his* new land.
His new home.

---

* *Reference to "Private Ryan," feeling guilty for the sacrifice of others [re. my parents], giving up excellent careers, in Europe, for me.*

The implied racial topic of the poem and its life-long consequences, are encapsulated in the French saying: "Au pays des aveugles, les borgnes sont les rois." (In the land of the blinds… the one-eyed seeing persons are kings."). This came to mind after the author's observation of the natural advantage of his "blending-in status," as a white person, upon his walking off the vessel from France, in the streets of a New York of the 1950's.[Nota bene: the change (in the poem) from being sighted to having only one nose.]

Off the Boat *

New York City...
a name made off the flatness of the paper of my geography books.
Its distance...
measured by width of a hand.
Its sounds...
part of the confusion of foreign words.

And frenetic strumming on "electrified" instruments.

A world
slightly "on this side" of the "Orson Well's: War of the worlds."

_____

And now... no more reprieve...

The tiny Statue of Liberty,
left in the morning fog, to the left of the boat.

No more reprieve....
Now on the streets...
in the bowels of metallic mastodons, from Detroit.

I walk... apparently invisible and somehow dispensed,
by my until now,
unremarkable white skin.

Protecting me
from the communality of the racial make-up of the street people
waking up... in this:
My first morning, in the new world.

New York city of the 1950's

* *One of my first version [and rare, first-person singular] of attempted poems, on this topic.*
[see notes]

Permanent Visa

The young man, was having his first American breakfast:
A thing of his movies' folklore:
James Dean and huge cars.

1950's and early days of T.V.
Sugary appeal of choices.
Cold milk on tasteless-flakes.
And sweetness… to blend.

No more tartines of real butter, and café au lait.
The world of his future, would be cleanly efficient.

———————————————

Under the smoothness of the fabric of his new home,
had been flattened the folds of collective guilt…

…learning later, in college,
that the fifth-generation black dinette-server
could… still,
have been showing his *temporary* visa.

White-European immigrant, going through New York (circa 1950's)

High School Hall Duty

Reasonable observers would agree:
By their high school, hall-duty days,
it was a motley crew.

Various thickness of prescription lenses.
Weird halting gaits.

Weak knees and heart.
Slightly deaf from sound concussions.
Over-inflated physical ability and humor.
Marital status in various parts of the spectrum.

At the end of their careers:
Most off-springs, mostly, well prepared for life.
Accomplished, good all-around citizens.

No… Clint Eastwood,
would not have attacked a hill with them:

But some time back, Uncle Sam…
had.

Pilots… navigators:
with a quarter-inch metal between them and the European soil.
Haggard, moribund, liberated concentration camps
looking up at their American tanks.

Shy, bookish, New England teacher:
Using his rudimentary French, for intel.
Had been left for dead, in a Normandie mortar hole.

They all went… ultimately did… and saw
Humans… do the inhuman… the unhuman.

The miracle was…
their gentle humanity: helping a hapless, new teacher.

*First-year high school teacher, learns details from recalcitrant ex-World War-Two G.I.s,
colleagues about their self-effacing heroism… now patrolling high school hallways.*

Saturday Night Predator

George Peppard, movie-star good looks.
And monetary lineage.

HE… would literarily come from "across the tracks."
A ten-minute single-minded stroll:
To a world, with shorter horizons and darker suns.

Smaller kitchens, and two-by-fours wooden stairs,
for living-room entertaining

A different world.

Local transport…
from fume-producing, hand-me-down buses.
Police to arrest drunk husbands.
Preachers to preach.
And barely-men, for Asian-wars.

Evolution knows nothing
of these man-made detours to betterment.

In the roulette-wheel of D.N.A,
Beauty in filth… *will* blindly produce beauty

And so, at his time slot,
our predator would take flight:

Late Saturday… summer afternoons.

Crossing diligently the high-speed tracks,
with his Wall-street style loafers, unsteady on the granite bed-rocks.

Whiffs of British Sterling,
and very white teeth.

He would slither through back yards and sport fields:
Appearing on *her* street…

For his evening of *more* privilege:
A look at her heavenly body.

And her eventual return, to the rest of us.

Rich, entitled teenage boy, wandering the "poor" neighborhood, and picking the prettiest girls. Then, to the World-War-Two type Quonset-dance-hall teenage center… and then, go back to his daddy's Yacht club.

Cultural, Sexual Étiquette

A night of insinuated torrid sex.
One last... verbally elegant, erotic reference
to the previous night's acrobatics.

A gentle pinch on his silk shirt.
A discreet tap on her lower back.

Return to the routine of routine.

But... for the quasi—nobility of the "bise:"

Its decorum.
The unbroken, natural movement toward each other!

The ceremonial.
The symbolic conclusion of things of the flesh.
A chiaroscuro of settings:
The bedroom's gentle shadows.
And the early morning urban light.

Cultural tradition "oblige", after a night of torrid sex, the airline cabin attendants kiss simply, and 'only' on the cheek: differentiating between the intimacy of one and the cultural of the other.
Inspired by, "Trois hommes et un couffin" ["Three men and a baby," in the original French version].

A Cultural Thing

It was definitely a "cultural" thing:
But without the annoyance of a bracelet on knitted sweaters.

.

Nor the vaporous expense
of a pricy *huile* de parfum from Grasse.

Or the vitreous lack of visceral warmth
of a bottle of grand cru.

Wanting instead, something
that would *reappear* into her present…

An evening… with her future current-friend(s):
Time to open the first of several bottles.

And the magic of space and time-travel,
through the chrome-solidity
of *his* corkscrew!

Taking her back to her kitchen on
that day after.
« C'est quoi ça ?» *
« Tu verras… »

And so…
it turned out as he had hoped.

Every once in a while:
Like an old Saint-Éxupéry-fifty francs note;
Like Yves Montand's Vinyl of Paris;
Like her favorite falafel at Sciences-Po.

Like the tinny sound
of a Romanesque church-bell in Montoroux.

Like one of her reaction to his non sequiturs:
"Quel con!" **
His presence… would re-invade her present.

Short but intense:
Like the smells of steamy couscous,
under naked light-bulbs at Saint Michel, on an August night.

* *What's this? /You'll see*
** *What an ass!*

Of Marie-Antoinette and Madonna

Spirits from another sphere.
Lost birds-without- borders…
tossed backwards by capricious headwinds.

Prisoners in some dark tale of evil step-mothers.
Forced to relive primitive-pasts of their sister-doppelgängers.

The pain being… not so much living the oppression.
The injustice. But sensing it.
Sensing them!

Your very flesh calling… on behalf of your sisters,
recalling… somehow…
intimacies: real or otherwise.

Reclaiming the pre-purgatory, exotic perfumes,
emanating from a carefree Eve.

The simple freedom of inquisitiveness.
The innate conviction that your other-self is living in freedom.

Every pulsating, vibrating cells of your skin:
Sensually, primordially… aware of *its* opposite.

Experiencing *the exact opposite*.
Sexual social repression.

Practically accused of Freudian visions,
when emotionally riding—fully naked—a white stallion.

All the time living,
through surrealistic alternate moments
and their dead reality.

Marie-Antoinette, Madonna, free-spirited women: the former having blossomed much too early for her era.

Beauty and savagery

Reflecting on the duality of societies and its individuals to produce both beauty and horrors: While witnessing the divine beauty of an orchestral piece by some flawed musicians, in the very walls that had witnessed historic tragedies.

Apparent human transfiguration of its *humanity,*
at its most visceral.
A momentary suppression of the finest,
most polished ideas and ideals.

A sort of perverted ritual
of the imposition-of-the-hands
by some Evil… for evil intent.

Humanity having turned its back
on its most differentiating make up from other species:

Its capacity of reflection, on *the notion of the beautiful*

Things, that are beheld.
Rather than explained.

Things, that touch *susceptible* souls.
Souls …
somehow opened to the sounds of color.
The weight of sunlight.
The humidity of a lover's bleeding heart.
And the heartless hissing of the lie.

All of the ingredients
Of life and living.

All of them captured
in the halting cascade of notes of the wood instruments.

A slight hesitation in the expected contact
with a drum skin.

A surprising masculinity from the brass.

And the incomparable "abandonment"
from a single note of the lead violin.

Reinforced romantic notions
of unbounded beauty, swirling around the orchestra.

———————————————

Maybe the Druids, the sorceresses....
-the mentally afflicted of history-

were, indeed, endowed with spirits of the beyond:
Better than our technologies: then and now.

artists, poets, musicians...
in their seventh floor Paris love-nets.
continued to be our conduits for the rest of us.
Even if temporarily full of flaws.

———————————————

This surrealistic visit to Berlin... to Vienna,
must have had a biblical, post-apocalyptic feel for survivors.

Grandiose churches and music academies
with the small pox of bullet holes.

The very place, for people, for the genesis
of untouchable beauty and viral violence.

———————————————

Was it, maybe late at night?
Beyond the artist's control, that the ink
traced magical arabesques on the rough parchment?

Musical notes, in the thick pointillistic formulae
of the creamy unctuousness of beauty.

Making, even its very own creator,
come out of his trance:

Still confused, but suspecting that something great had entered

the solidity of his reality:
In doppelgangers of music.
As reincarnations of his intimacies on music paper.

─────────────

While in the concerto hall,
every minute, of every moment, of magistral execution
is under the director's baton.

Surges of commands from his index:
Like some Renaissance deity.

Inciting *from* the orchestra,
the language of the gods.

From that orchestra.
From that stage.
On that day.

The one… with musicians from
the disparate backgrounds, ethnicities and worries.

Various flaws and prejudices:
Miraculously cleansed by the searing heat of beauty.

Heteroclite gathering.
Unified from chaos.

If only, for the length of the musical piece
The director.
The focus.

The one with the raised index. The commanding nod of the chin.
The glance… toward the wind instruments.
His timely lean of the torso.

Multiplied to perfection by the studious submission.
The response of the instruments.
All for the greater good.

That is …
Raising from the stellar dust that is Earth,
nothing more aggressive…
than the beautiful.

———————————————

Waking up from the trance of the *fable*.
The noise of a book falling on the floor:

On the wrinkled headline of a newspaper, reads:
"First violin leaves chair, to quiet sex scandal with trumpetist."

Witnessing the antithetical felling of the quasi-divine music of an orchestral ensemble in a former axis nation.

Little Girls... and Wars

Hard working. Callused hands.
A giant protector of his family two-bedroom ranch.

An idyllic start for this girl:
Youth has ways of smoothing life's imperfections.

The family dog acting each morning with the same enthusiasm upon
running to the brook.

Life lived, in its own cosmic laws:
Reality for her, started at the tree and rock by the road.

No need to invent fiction:
A summer's hot afternoon, distant bells ringing
and her favorite biscuits browning in the oven...
would do.

She did not sense the frigid winds of adulthood invade.
Nor the toxicity of losing innocence.

There were no biblical pillars at the end of the yard.
But they were there.
The danger was there!

Their granite skin:
Pale-shade... of things dead.
Unpolished... mat...mineral frigidity.

Not luscious like the pregnant red-apples
of her father's orchard on the hill.

What would a youngster know of truths?

She... must have somehow
crossed an imaginary line by the flower bed.

Some evil pollen must have been spread by a sorcerer:
She was now much taller than the hutch.
"My father used to measure me here,"
she whispered to herself.

He had come back, full of medals,
having killed other men.

But somehow, she never did not sense her expulsion
from the Garden of Eden.

Little girl's memories of her gentle, green-thumb father, emotionally destroyed by his Viet Nam experience.

An Eye... For an Eye.

A parable

In honor of the Amazon Women:
A targeted law:
A remedy... to somewhat appease the past victims.
And focus on a somewhat satisfying solution.

It could even involve music:
Vestals, appropriately dressed in transparent Egyptian cotton:
Wielding appropriately bejeweled, very sharp knives.

A child of Hammurabi's code:
It would not bring back the use of the original eye,
but strongly remind the offender of his deed.

It would remind him during any future occasional need,
to use his own corresponding part of his anatomy,
for any other purpose than emptying his bladder.

Thus, the ceremony would conclude
with a good grip on the end of a precious shaft,
and a swift slice.

With enough religious references,
this activity could be as merry as Christmas.

The barbary of the excision of women.

Ritual

The persistent horrors of female-genital mutilation.

At the incestuous crossroad
of the cultural
and oppressive.

The rite of passage
and the torture.

The traditional
and the imposed.

The silence and injustice
toward a little girl's trust.

The perversion
of parental
and societal authority.

Lie the future moments
of denied intimate joys assaulted by
frigid concepts.

Divine presence

Cosmological sciences... seen as no more than modern-day, of what was considered, mythology in the past: that is, humanity trying to represent itself in its earthly setting. Watching YouTube high level calculations by the brightest minds, with themes such as "how big is the universe and can we have come from nothing?

It must have been communicated by the quiet,
most aloof member of the group....
Early beginnings of early humankind.

An explanation for the frustrating disappearance of this "thing" in the sky.
Source of warmth and light:
A good presence, among so many deadly ones!

And so... began surrealistic...
escapist tales of the inexplicable, mystical object:
A very human answer, to what apparently concerned only humans.

The white robes, of high priests under sunbaked Greek marble...
seem to have given way to corduroy-clad professors.

Beauty of the equations!
The sterility of an academic lecture hall,
The white board, somehow transforming itself into the pinkish flesh
from Italian Renaissance artists.

Having filled the emptiness of the universe
with opiates of mythologies.
With human-size avatars
easily manipulated in space and time ...by the arts and the artist.

A feeling of accompanied confusion:
The nervous intelligence of our professor's hand on ours,
like that of a steady Virgil.

And then... the beacon:
The emotional home of human...tactile life.

The something out of nothing.
Our very own *Beatrice*!
... the pregnant eternity of a woman's glance.

And the echoing presence...
... the omnipresence of remnants of rationalism:
Whispering deadly scenarios:
That of meeting intelligence in the far future
just a clueless as we are...

the elegant arabesques of multi-dimensional calculus
relegated to its rightful place:
Next to our bodies, made of inert stellar dust.

Post script: university lecture on advanced cosmology; sitting three seats to the right, the stand-in for Beatrice, has just smiled at me!

The Constructed Gods

The constructed gods and ethics of mankind
have led us to what we interpret as a sentient conscience;
Awareness…
of our cosmological luck…
of the improbability of the Earth…
our living on it…
and our evolution.

Cosmology has given us
elegant equations:
None of them hinting at a divine intent.

The emptiness of the theater of the absurd,
still, and will ever, be in place.

The Old Testament is indeed
like many of the best of our literatures:

That is, in its fictional way,
describing the Truth.

The earth with its clean drinkable water
is simply, a secular heaven:
A glorious, statistical, noble miracle.

and we are losing it:
The Greeks and their grumpy gods told us so.

Thus, spoke the righteous among us.

Perceptible Silence

To Pierre-Auguste Renoir, who hopefully died with visions of his paintings in mind.

Moments of majesty, such as the *setting sun* on the ocher of the
Hassan Mosque, next to its green Atlantic.

The aromatic oils of the maritime pines, like wisps of burned incense,
during cemetery pilgrimages, north of Marseille.

Proustian reconstruction of *maternal presence,*
with every bite of garlic and provençale-oil brandade de morue.

Dizzying twists of the Corniche above the crystalline Mediterranean,
with the call of Italy, through early, warm evening mist, to the east.

All this expansive canvas, spread over his soul:
Suddenly penetrated by memories of her aggressive glance.

Eyes full of ambivalent femininity.
Seemingly, containing remnants from primitive evolution.

Time and space, handled like primordial cave-mud,
Due to the heat of artistic fervor… in order to regain both.

It had been just a simple, natural, peaceful reflection upon this universe:
From within the routine of a morning coffee.

A universe… coldly indifferent to human consciousness.
Now…
swaddling him like a new-born.

All these contradictions.
All the noises of life.

The silences of the void of space:
Unresolved, in spite of all the equations of the laws of cosmology
and the *improbability of existence's… very existence.*

And then…
as proof of humanity's indominable, gentle strength:
The non-computable world of humanity's imagery of language and
metaphors.

For,
as though to contradict the laws of cosmology,
there was this *"perceptible silence"*
of the flutter of a black butterfly's wings coming through the
garden window…
into his dying soul.

Lyrical moments in an artist's life. (inspired by Pierre-August Renoir's last years)

Disappearing In Front of His Eyes

She was a timeless presence, across the frigidity of a cafeteria;
Protected by a layered, organic complexity in this setting of efficiency.

He recognized hints of reserved passion,
Discernable through her gentle febrility.

Making her quasi-magical appearance in his life,
heartbreakingly precious.

There was… already… a transparence in her presence across the table:
Tempting him to accidently brush his hand against her coat.

Touch… the salt-shaker after her:
In the hopes of sensing remnants… of her heat.

Time and space coldly conspiring,
in front of his helpless senses:
Nullifying her solidity.

"I only have a few minutes." « *Je n'ai que quelques minutes* »
Seeing her between his train and her plane.

Of Greek Gods Among Us

In the tumultuous world of Mythology,
with all the very human emotions of its gods and deities,
with the disabused characters of that divine comedy:

Their petty jealousies. The regally imposed excruciating pains.
The various reasons for torturing their confederacy.

With all sorts of arbitrary tests of allegiances.
And then…
Such victims as Sisyphus and Prometheus,
for doing and thinking of … *things*… human.

They were both, lower members of the club
of overinflated egos and powers:
Therefore, more deserving of punishments.

Secondary line of pretenders to higher status.
More easily paraded for their disrespect:
With eternal physical or emotional chains of containment against rocks.

Perfect offering, as religious peons, for power gains.

These two had dared rebel and then gloriously failed.
Lawlessness was indeed exhibited.
Their torturers… the gods of gods had names.
Their Heavens were not empty,
like ours.

They were familiar:
One… Zeus by name.
All properly evil.

The verdicts:
Meaningless eternal manual labor.
And endless food for vultures.

Yes! These judges had names.
Faces.
And like the defendants, had their well-known shameful flaws.
Disgusting deeds and secrets… to hide and bury.

Thus, Sisyphus and Prometheus *knew* their judges:
More akin to neighborhood *collaborator*-bullies:

They knew the source of their pain:
Could cry out their names!

Could it have been some measure of satisfaction,
(whispering to themselves, during their labor)

"My torturer is inflicting torture on his own image?"

Long before Freud…
these insecure deities… "*projected!*"

———————————————

There… lies the grandeur of modern moralists like Camus:
Camus surrounded by
his own mythological creation:
Docteur Rieux.

And all these *absurdists, existentialists, nihilists*
and others of the same blue-blooded universe.

Thinkers and creators
of similar self-reflecting philosophical spheres.

Thus Rieux… was forced to find his way, without the *good book.*
In a silent setting.
With an unconcerned, absentee landlord.

Completely unphased
by the flow of normal human kindness.

But rather, the blindly inhuman.
Nonhuman.

Super deities… seemingly finding satisfaction
—and the borderline arousal—
upon inflicting pain.
Warped… pathological, viral-infected pain.
As many and any of the others,
found in the annals of history.

Sisyphus and Prometheus could blame the gods
But…
Docteur Rieux… Camus… and their ilk… could not.
Cannot!

Suffering instead,
with no expectation of even a glance from the universe.
Nothing and no-one to do it.

Nothing and no-one, even caring about their agonies:
Like the ones found on museums walls.

Sadism is a mirrored world:
The torturer and its victim.

Suffering in a god-less cosmos is guiltless.
And worse… not redeeming.

No sainthood. No titles of martyrdom.
No fame… good or bad.

Secular moralists have no eternity in their future.
Therein lie their true glory. Their nobility,

A sainthood with no true recompense.
No true value. No true price.

Nothing…
but the warmth of the Mediterranean sun.
The salt-water droplets blanching the curls of black hair.
The reddish rocks near the dark-blue Mediterranean, off of Tipasa.
And wisps,
left in her wake, of flowers and flesh. *

To those survivors of the horrors, atrocities, catastrophes of human history, who have lost and never regained faith, in any faith. And who, nevertheless, acted with humanity and determination toward their Other... this poem is dedicated.

Sisyphus and Prometheus knew of the dead-end of their fate and still persisted.

Camus and all secular-saints do not even have the satisfaction of challenging an almighty, all-knowing, scient entity.

* Paraphrase of Camus' description, of Marie walking by Camus/the narrator, on the beach.

Kansas Farm

"... He called for his mother, before expiring..."

He died…
Five thousand miles from his Kansas farm;
It was where…
the spinster teacher had told her classes of realities
on the other side of the horizon.
About…
"The curvature of the earth"
on the other side of the farmers' fields.

That was when his boyhood world
had begun to be invaded by unwanted truths.

———————————

Little did he know… that the cold metallic feel
of the rifle of boot-camp,
had been a precursor
of the amoral solidity of evil,
waiting at the end of the bus ride to indoctrination.

Did he have visions of his mother's Sunday mornings apple pies,
when he returned to pastoral peace?

On the command deck of an assault naval ship off the Normandie coast: Ear-drums perforated by the impact of a direct hit; an officer can barely make sense of the seaman's words. The latter is missing the bottom half of his body… crying for his mother. (loosely inspired by real events, as recalled by a comrade).

Skin Deep Stigmata

Spreading rumors, from a thatch hut in the village:
The birthing mother's painful cries
gave way to the witnessing family's horrified silence.

From between the sweat and blood-soaked thighs,
squirmed a beautifully-formed, baby-boy.

A spectacularly healthy being,
in the presence of a quasi-biblical retinue of farm animals.

With his father's questioning oblique glances.
And years of social agony
Toward the other.

Reflections on a documentary about the difficulties faced by Albino children in Africa

Elephant Orphanage

When all is said and done with humanity,
visitors will come to this place and say:
"This is where it all started."

So, was it entered,
in the logs of a future space traveler.

This apparent rocky sphere, third from a dying star,
will have seen its days.

Soil samples and analyses,
will show remnants of a luxurious past under succeeding,
very advanced ones.

The "would be poet" on the scientific team
would lyrically record:

"It was the equivalent of pioneers stumbling
into a heretofore unknown thriving valley.

And… within generations,
Pollute it all with death.

A prodigal-son re-enactment,
on a cosmic scale."

The scene taking place on unearthed evidence
of an elephant grave yard, on what was once,
the birth of humanity:
Africa.

Reflections on a program about an African man, on the outskirts of his village, diligently caring and washing orphaned, baby elephants.

Who Needs Hades?

Cosmological sciences... seen as no more than a modern-day, of what was once considered, mythology. Humanity's attempt to represent itself in this, its earthly setting. Watching high level presentations of calculations by the invited brightest minds: With themes such as, "How big is the universe?" and "Can we have come from nothing?"

It must have been communicated
—by the quiet, most aloof member of the group—
in the infancy of humankind.

Their *explanation*
for the frustrating disappearance of this "thing" in the sky:
Source of warmth and light.

Such a good presence, among so many deadly ones!

And so... began *sur*-realistic... escapist tales of the inexplicable,
mystical object:
A very human answer, to what seemed to concern only humans.

––––––––––––

Then the eventual white robes, of high priests
under sunbaked Greek marble...
having seemingly given way to corduroy-clad professors:
And the beauty of their equations,

In the sterility of an academic lecture hall,
in the day-dreams of students.

White boards, somehow transforming themselves
into the pinkish flesh from Italian Renaissance paintings.

Cultures trying to fill the emptiness of the universe
with opiates of mythologies,
and human-sized avatars.

All easily manipulated, in space and time,
by artists and their arts.

A feeling of mathematical and philosophical confusion,
accompanying the nervous intelligence of our professor
—his hand guiding ours—
Like that of a steady Virgil.

And then... the beacon:
The emotional home of human...tactile life.
Safely away from the "something out of nothing"...
our Beatrice...
... the pregnant eternity of a friendly glance.

And still... this echoing presence:
The omnipresence of remnants of rationalism.

Whispering deadly scenarios:
That of meeting *intelligence...* someday, in the far future
just as clueless as we are!

All these elegant arabesques of multi-dimensional calculus,
relegated to its place:
Next to our bodies made of inert stellar dust.

Post script: Sitting three seats to the right, in this sciences lecture-hall, a stand-in for today's Beatrice, has just smiled at me!

Pleasant Valley School

The custodian would, respectfully,
make *his* noise in the hallway:

His usual way…
to remind the venerable English teacher of quitting time.

That afternoon… the last…
she had, instead, been waiting for the jingling of his keys.

Like the captain of her ship,
she would make sure to be the last to leave, on this final occasion.

Carrying her precious cargo
of her early "number-two" pencil, essays.

Fading light-blue covers:
Such as… of a now-pediatrician's first attempts,
to describe his love for his Springer Spaniel.

She stepped into the empty parking lot,
which had strangely started to shrink, in her gaze.

An elementary school.
Now empty:
With an impatient bush…
already invading, the once busy driveway.

The closing of a local elementary school.

Organic Complexity of Hers

Pages from a personal mythology

It was the multitude of uncontrollable visions,
flashing in his mind as he approached her group.

It was her seeming indifference toward her own qualities.
A natural ease of sophistication:
Like observing a seamless feline movement.

Her verbal cues,
adding to his apparently sleepy primordial reactions.

She was, in this corner of the reception,
her own microcosm of riches of the senses:
Existing in a single planet.

An organic emotional complexity,
whose secret recipe she would... later...
in a confessional tone, hint to offer.

He never did... dare to accept...
somehow fearing...
her entering a universe...
that destroys muses...
... Reality.

And so, when the end drew near.
To the last instants of their relationship.
With her lips showing a perceptible trembling.

In the grip of a *confessional* exhaustion.
At that very extreme... he put an end to the agony;
Bringing his left index finger to her lips.

Stopping her words.
Not wanting to hear the recipe for her complexity.

Afraid that he might, in a moment of weakness,
reveal IT in his own lyricism.

But would rather die,
having had hints of a carnal knowledge reserved for only the gods.

"I could not help but treat her as a deity in an otherwise silent universe"

Orgasmatron

Troublesome human ancestor,
for this impeccably dressed Wall Street executive:
The most successfully aggressive, of the investment group.

The envy of the new M.B.A.s recruits:
Michael Douglas good-genes: For all around success.

Seemingly… feline peripheral vision,
for would-be competition and sneak attacks.
Quasi-animal grace in this… his sixtieth-floor habitat.

Voted most likely, by the back-office pool,
to propagate his seeds, after end-of-quarter meetings.

Society's natural self-selection, for survival-genes:
Making our Italian suit-clad finance wizard,
a perfect doppelganger of his prehistoric,
hirsute, and very muscular ancestor.

Could the installation of a company-Orgasmatron,
bring civilized behavior?
Not unlike the Greek women of Athens and Sparta,
Redirecting masculine aggressivity.

Orgasmatron: fictional orgasm-inducing device in the 1973 film "Sleeper."

La belle Ferronnière

"Never had he beheld such a magnificent brown skin, so entrancing a figure, such dainty, transparent fingers. He stood gazing in wonder at her work-basket as if it was something extraordinary. What was her name? Where did she live and what sort of life did she lead? What was her past? He wanted to know what furniture she had in her bedroom, the dresses she wore, the people she knew; even his physical desire for her gave way to a deeper yearning, a boundless, aching curiosity." (L'Éducation Sentimentale) Gustave Flaubert, describing the process of his character falling in love.

Impressionable young man.
Malleability of soul and beliefs.

City of lights:
Genesis of "Une education sentimentale."

Ferment of
quasi revolution of '68 Paris streets.

Overstimulation of all the senses:
Tastes. Smells.
Mores:
"Je t'aime… moi non plus".

———————————————

Post army-draft and leftovers of emotional disasters.
Time for reflection.
And emphasis on *living*.

The appeal of the stately Louvre,
with its apparent aura of quiet space.

A sort of encyclopedic voyage to a past.
If not peaceful, at least, solidly categorized.

———————————————

Italy. The quattrocento.
His very own blood-line: Speaking to him,
in the unctuous layers of oil paints.

A magical cacophony:
A building dedicated to a quieted history,
in the middle of a tortured present.
Place Saint Michel,
and his own bruised emotional ego.

Then…
in la Galerie de la Joconde… on the far-left wall.
There *she* is: the other one!
La Belle Ferronnière!

His "man-of-the world" reputation,
reduced to a little boy's sentimentality:
"She has the same glance as hers!"
He tearfully murmurs.

Once again, in front of those huge…
bottomless… brown eyes, of his past!

Gradation,
from the safe-familial, to the carnal.

From benevolence, all the way to Faustian temptation:
Smiling at him!

And… somehow… all was well in his heart:
Knowing, that the artist had, openly,
immortalized *that* glance.

"La belle Ferronnière": painting, of unclear provenance, but associated to Leonardo de Vinci, of a woman wearing a metallic hair pin: Hence "Ferronnière." Nota bene: At the time set for the poem (in the same exhibit room as the Mona Lisa), the Ferronnière was about fifty feet to the left of the Mona Lisa; but it was, instead, the unexpected, appearance the former's eyes, that made a moving, lasting, and very personal impression on the narrator.
(Post scriptum: the author considers the epigraph-quote from Flaubert, as the most realistic, most concise and yet most romantic description of falling in love.)

Macaque Motherhood

The mother, with a quick and precise gesture,
picked a small shoot of a particular plant:

Placing it near the snout and lips of her infant.

In a seamless movement,
the mother and child walked to the quieter back.

At last look, the baby was munching.
The mother, seated, was gently using her powerful legs
for the youngster's balance.

The years of studies, in infectious diseases,
had no explanation for the enormous tears
burning her cheeks.

Post-doctoral student, in primate studies, who has just found out she is expecting a baby-girl.

Intimate Mythology

They had said their goodbyes at *their* corner.
Place Saint Michel; "by the bridge."

Stigmata of her glance upon him.

But what a glance!
After all these years,
all his words… his art… represented what… the artist…
at his heroically best… and lonely best…
reconstructs:
A human capture of time and space.

While these many years later:
Still realizing that he had left the best of himself in her embrace.

Whispering to himself:
"So… this is how and why humanity turned so seamlessly to
mythologies":

Flawed divinities, flawed souls.
Made-up avatars, who have known perfection:

And are now wandering in a wasteland of their making.

Lady in white

Like being visited by the night nurse:
Feverish. Mouth full of sand.
Dying to acknowledge her presence...
And to later, tell about her!

Multi-layered mirage:
Salvation. Irresistible sensuality.
Untouchable aura.

Phantasms of early calls of sensuality,
incarnated in a sternness of silky white:
Covering hints of *modelé* of flesh.

All... dutifully repressed in the annals of Freudians myths.
And yet...how could a dream remain unreal
during the awaken hours of decades?

Evening outdoor party in the luxurious warmth of youth.
Quartier du Val Fleuri, Port Lyautey/Kénitra, Morocco (circa 1950's)

From author's note book:
> *A lady in white lives in Morocco...*
> *surrounded by blood-red cannac.*
> *She is attended by furtive breaths...*
> *from fears of chasing the vision.*
> *She had appeared the way youth creates magic:*
> *With the nonchalance of clueless moments*
> *Bursting into spectacular hints of the future.*

Imprinted By Its Presence

Like ducklings...

IT... had simply... always been there:
Behind the transparency of the floating, living-room cotton.

A perfect imprinting, based on a nonjudgmental love,
that only the innocence of youth instills.

Made of simple red clay and eternal blue skies:
It had the ingredients, so naturally captured by youth...

... Later inflaming poetic passions...

Made of the ocher of its walls
and crystalline of its nights,

that could...
unfortunately, only travel in his heart.

La Tour Hassan [The Hassan Tower].

Nonjudgmental imprinting [like ducklings], on the author as a youngster, associated with things and persons that were "simply... just there during youth."

Solinga family [living-room photograph] of view from Salé, across the river Bou Regreg toward Rabat, Morocco.

The Hassan Tower (Mosque): "... had the noble secular beauty of an ochre solar-dial, in a quadrant of eternal blue." (From author's notes.)

See also in notes, "Maman Barka", regarding her influence in the author's life.

Marqué de sa Présence

Comme des canetons...

Elle avait, tout simplement, toujours été là :
Derrière la transparence cotonneuse flottante des rideaux du salon.

Une parfaite gravure, dans un amour sans arrière-pensée,
Que seule l'innocence de la jeunesse peut insuffler.

Faite de terre glaise et de nuées bleues éternelles :
Elle avait les ingrédients attirés par la jeunesse...

... qui enflammeront plus tard des passions lyriques

Construites dans l'ocre de ses murs
et le cristal de ses nuits

qui ne pouvaient
malheureusement, que voyager à travers le cœur.

Gravée sur ma jeunesse : La vue de notre salon, de l'autre rive du fleuve Bou Regreg, de la
Tour Hassan, Rabat, Maroc.
La noble beauté séculaire d'une horloge solaire en ocre, dans un quadrant de bleu éternel.

Pale blue Dot
(Part one)
Desert lovers

A fable

Telagh, Algeria

He would call her *"mon agate bleue"*:
The name of his favorite marble.

The one, that would allow itself
to display its finest intricate, mineral structures.

He had remarked, that she had the same, strikingly uncommon,
turquoise eyes:
She would claim, traces of an invading Roman soldier.

Another, unwelcomed invader
in her unwelcoming Rif mountains.

But like some-want-to-be woman-Titan figure,
She found, in the arid rocks of the bled,
a limitless spiritual strength.

A daughter of shepherds,
she was *made* of the landscape:

In her glance, an apparent thirst
for the non-religious, wild open spaces.

Seemingly, always looking beyond the restrictions
of any borders, made by mankind.

———————————————

He was the *Rumi*
The Northern invader. The Visigoth.
The Other.

But also, a malcontent,
that troubles societies' order:
No matter how imperial or venerated.

But…once in a while… it happens:
Life and living delivers itself…
body and soul to…
life and living.

———————————————

Through mostly their glances and their flesh,
their respective reflections, spoke of unverbalized,
pre-paradisiac, non-paradisiac… natural love.

Young and pliable enough:
Still free from dogmas and artifices of civilizations and cultures.

In the remaining heat from the desert rocks,
their emotions were incarnated into the crimson Maghreban sunsets of
billions of sand-particles.

That night,
under the nuptial candles made of stars:
Written and oral commandments, from various gods were ignored.

Simple goodness
must have, enviously smiled upon the couple:
Sprinkling amoral dust over them.

Turning the grit found at the bottom of cultures and religions,
Into its cosmological antithesis:

The unctuous cream of tactile human happiness.

Inspired by the author's continuing reflections upon looking at Voyager1's, photograph of the Earth, 4,7 billion miles away (the size if a single pixel): Noting, "Somewhere on that pale blue dot," beings, with self-awareness intelligence, have killed for religion, skin color and land."

Pale Blue Dot
(Part Two)

When she gave birth…
the baby's skin… as if remembering the desert sand,
brought forth, magical wisps of warmth, from the Scirocco
and shy breezes from the Atlantic.

Like an adoration from a biblical scene,
the event, gathered around the medical professionals,
used to the inorganic, white-sterility, of hospital sheets.

This new life… a glorious union of so many currents of loves and hates…
was like a massive… blackhole of forgiveness:

Absorbing in that tiny, precocious buddle of cries and kicks,
Absorbing… all and everything…
that humans had spewed, hiding the way back to paradise:

That baby…
was the symbol that even mythologies can, at times,
ask for forgiveness for their unforgiving Canonic demands.

Jean-Yves in front of the Mellah and souk of Salé (across the street). It is a fortified city from which the Barbary Coast boats would sail out to the ocean, from massive gates.

Jean-Yves, with his mother, at the Tour Hassan, in Rabat: an unfinished mosque intended to be the biggest in the Islamic world.(c1195)

The Tour Hassan (seen from the family living room). it is on the opposite bank of the river Bou Regreg, in Rabat

Barka (in djellaba) and Jean-Yves, in Salé.

Barka

"I would rather 'disappear' behind Barka's persona" (from author's notebook)

In his old leather, university briefcase,
on the top shelf, behind unused cook books:
Her image in a black and white photo.

The intensity of the Maghreban sun: still its main character.

A side comment… about the Moroccan cumin in the dish…
And a… viscerally induced synesthesia.

From his youth:
Smells, from the neighborhood souk.

The evening "kesra" bread from the oven.
"Bread" … that for him, was no less than:
"humanity's apogee over the animal kingdom."

She is back…
her vaporous curves, selfishly hiding behind the white, pudic,
cotton-screen of a flowing summer djellaba.

His pubescent glance
trying to interpret the language of this unknown universe.

As though in magical unison,
the setting is scented in a duality of the dangerous attraction
of the engorged, crimson prickly-pears.

Near Sidi Moussa,
in the rocky privacy of a cave overlooking a minuscule beach:
Beyond all social and religious commandments,
joyfully ignoring conventions:

Youth did, what it does best:
Create the privacy of time-warps, where dreams help escape reality.

Far… far away from the artifice of smart technologies.
or the mind-numbing, servile equations of mathematics…

… THE EXPANSE OF THE UNIVERSE
allowed itself to be held in their grasp:
IT…
could, indeed, be tamed, appeased… by the simple stroke of fingers tips.
The closing of eye lids.

―――――――――――

That hot afternoon, with the green Atlantic,
the yellow bled… and watchful presence of a Marabout, as witnesses…

their untouched flesh
would be properly sacrificed on nature's altar.

Not with ceremonials, incantations, or burning incent.
Not imposed oaths:

But rather… elementary, life-giving, organic sighs.

Youthful offerings, on the tabernacle to Mediterranean gods:
Humanity's own carnal eternity.

―――――――――――

From shards, chiseled in Grecian marble:
The one reserved for its divinities.

From uncontrollable outbursts.
Like escaped spirits from the soul:
Also found in the gentle afternoon darkness of curtains.

Like a priceless statuette, nervously broken on a Parisian parquet floor.
Like beads of salty sweat eagerly tasted.

Like a quick, last glance toward her climbing *away* into a taxi.
Like envying the coffee rim caressed by her blood-red lips…

… still… and always..
in the artist's… any artist's…

this recurrent fear:
The need to fill the present... with pieces of its past.

Had Barka... and others like her...
stopped to exist after the camera-shutter's closing?

Had she not fully reappeared since this tiny black and white photograph?
In the similarity of Others?
What part of them had also been *fictions of reality*?

Art and the artist...
and the insatiable, creative void:
To be filled by the only currency capable of capturing time...

that is... lawless... cosmologically untethered,
human... *sentient consciousness.*

Having bounced images of his muse
off the walls of tiny Parisian hotels:
He reconstructed her.

Like a little boy breaking his new watch:
"to see where time comes from":
The artist takes apart pieces of moments, to reconstruct new elements,
hoping to sooth the longing of icons of happiness.

Having left Barka... as he looked at her receding image
in the oval of the rear of his father's Volkswagen,
he would honor their nuptials
their continuing existence
through the fiction of their love.

They had not seen each other since youth:
But reality has only control over minerals and asteroids.
For... once in a while,
the universe liberates parts of itself.

Giving art and artists
poetic discretion over cosmic randomness.

―――――――――――――

Barka… never did leave him, after that afternoon.
The cold atoms… themselves,
in a gigantic divine dispensation, had insulated these two lives
from the imposition of linear time.

Her glance…
full of the hazel reflections of the symbolic richness of her Berber blood,
had been the last thing he remembered before…
making *one… out of two.*

From author's notes: "Re: Barka,"

Re-reading my notes, on other poems with their excruciating rawness, excavating into the rich and deep dirt of undisclosed… and or… undisclosable knowledge of confessional moments [to the author/writer's voice], this particular poem… this figure… this setting… presented another situation for a curtain of modesty to explore the author-text… reality-fiction relationship. And of course, I returned to my notes on Roland Barthes.
The reconstruction of this person of my youth, was akin to her presence having come suddenly in contact with the proper liquid to add to the lifeless powder of the past.

I opted to still call her "Barka" [the same as the real person] and not a literary template, substitute, as I have done for others in my work.

I like who she was and still is to me. I like the sound; I like how I had to rebuild her from family pictures and souvenirs.

This is what Poland Barthes hints to, in particular, in his splendid analysis if the "Death of the author," as well as the one of "Sarrasine," by Honoré de Balzac. In other words: Who is... and what is this author? And what is his or her relationship to the artistic "creation."

"Barka" would give an insight of how my poetry develops itself: She was somehow, like anti-matter; I could lose myself in contact with my creation. Her artistic persona could, therefore, "be dictated by her!"

Her presence in my text was a difficult one: Not "her" per say or my affection for her... but rather as a real-politick, geopolitical symbol of someone who could define... me... the author and the person.

I therefore, affirm [as I did in my thesis on the Maghreb] my prerogative to choose lyricism and beauty, as guides concerning the ethics and realism of my written world.

And so... a conversation about Morocco: With family members and those black and white photographs... and the glue that the creative act often uses... "the past" ... and its remaining pieces, were all that I needed.

I had been by haunted by innate contradictions in this muse's persona: intimate with some details and only vagueness for others. Suspicions and shadows of hints about other ingredients of her make-up, that, as a child, I did not know (... care or need to know).

I had to choose early on: create a fiction based on reality or chance getting more, and needless "grit" ... that had been suggested by family members.

I chose, instead, to disappear [if not die] behind Barka's persona: "No longer the focus of creative influence, the author is merely a "scriptor" (a word Barthes uses expressively to disrupt the traditional continuity of power between the terms "author" and "authority"). The scriptor exists to produce but not to explain the work and "is born simultaneously with the text [underline by j-y.s.] is in no way equipped with a being preceding or exceeding the writing, [and] is not the subject with the book as predicate." Every work is "eternally written here and now," with each re-reading, because the "origin" of meaning lies exclusively in "language itself" and its impressions on the reader. (Wikipedia: "The death of the author")

Early Spring

It had been a severe winter.
A non-descript town in the middle of Europe.

But nature recognizes its deep swells of the call for the rebirth of things:
Shy early spring sprouts.
Hints of gentleness from the south west.

And so… following their ritual,
the returning birds had already paired.
Nested… and been caring for future generations.

A sweet cacophony of uncontrollable chirping,
preparing for the continuity of life for the living,
in this corner of the globe:

The sounds…
reaching into a nearby railroad car…
and a young man…
trying to turn free… his soul.

Oswiecim, Poland, early 1940

"An Espresso… and Some Romance."

Coffeehouse in quaint New England town.

The Universal
often finds its roots in the mundane.

Could it be, that this is how sacred grounds…
become so…
by the unpretentious continuity they contain?

Among the steamy vapors of cappuccinos,
You could overhear:
Muted confessions of spousal infidelities.
A daughter's still grieving paternal lost.
Heartbreaking revelation of "special child" syndrome.
Failure to get into Med school.

All these pieces of very deep lives exposed:
Without fanfare. Without headlines.

In a setting: unpretentious.
Bare: in the image of a Greek stage.

Assortment of characters,
"entering front door."

Announced
by the wobble of the handle.

Unburdening themselves
between the noise of the street and their walk to a table.

A truly 'living' theater.

A commedia dell arte, with its recurrence
of sad and comic masks.

The stage full of its brand of eternal pathos.

Confirming every time and every day,
that life is indeed a stage.

Excruciating stories of youthful, needy souls;
Rejected by clueless parents.

Miserable, still unformed, late middle-age adults:
Still adrift in childhood.

Recurring, troublesome episodes of hard, multiple realities:
From lack of psychotropic medications.

The sad beginnings of signs of decrepitude,
in the nicest, underserving souls.

And their suffering, the double injustice
of their self-awareness!

All and everything… happening,
between the title page of the omnipresent local newspaper,
and the obituary of a friend.

But life has its gentle reminders of its own presence
in the microcosm of these fifteen tables:

"Hey people! She has accepted to get married where we met!"

They say…
that there were tears, around the majestic, polished-steel,
Italian, coffee-machine:
Acting as an altar.

First Came Her Name

First came her name…
curving echoes, overheard,
in the cement and glass setting of a maternity ward.

It had been the result
of a romantic mother's insistence.

It must have, all the while,
shyly existed at the magical intersection
—of the carnal and ethereal—
in her maternal being.

A girl… as yet unformed:
Between the signifier and its signified.

A pinkish innocent new life from life;
and its later sensual and sexual evolution.

A first name…three syllables…
Followed by the nobility of an organic combination of traits.

A first name:
One…
with femininity… sensuality and presence.

Tomorrows.
Joys and beauty.

Moments upon moments of time-stopping embrace.
A mythological grail:
Giving human form to the idea.

All of this new world. And many others:
At their *genesis.*

To eventually appear to him
in freezing-morning lecture hall.

An appearance. Now… fully formed:
Three seats to his right.
In sleepy morning philosophy lecture.

Taking place in the *magic-inducing fumes of the day's topic:*
"Grecian thought of the ideal."

Reflections of an un-apologetically romantic young freshman, upon visiting his new girlfriend's parents and being told by her mother about romantic notions of Hawaii and hence, her daughter's uncommon first name.

From Evolution… to Prejudice

The evenhanded discrimination of the innocent.
Ironic reaction… of modern mankind…
to the children… of its children.

Like new immigrants in their new land,
often trying to divest themselves of their old skins.

Under the diminishing solar presence of northern latitudes:
Their very flesh, had forgotten its past.

But, from time to time
and according to hazards of generics,
pesky chromosomes, along for the ride,
reminding the village dwellers of a danger in their midst:

Some sort of devilish sign of the universal
"other" …
in the hut next door.

Television program about Albano children in Africa: Anthropological study of recorded attitude of African blacks toward albino children.

Heartbreaking sadness of study in African village of marginalization of an albino youngster in Africa. [not "mixed-race" but most likely the result of random DNA sequencing]

"I Only Have a Few Minutes."

She was a timeless presence, across the frigidity of a cafeteria;
Protected by a layered organic complexity in this setting of efficiency.

He recognized hints of reserved passion,
discernable through the febrility of her soul.

Making her quasi-magical appearance, in his life:
Heartbreakingly precious.

There was a transparence in her very presence across the table:
Tempting him to accidently brush her hand, her coat.

Touch the salt-shaker after her:
In the hopes of sensing remnants… of her heat.

Time and space coldly conspiring,
in front of his helpless senses:
Nullifying her solidity.

Seeing her between his train and her plane: « Je n'ai que quelques minutes ».

Brilliant Minds With Bad Manners

Not unlike telling a patient of his dead-end prognosis.
Yes... life...
but does he understand
what his very own existence means?

Life... *or whatever its very opposite is.*

Life... but...
for no apparent reason and no particular purpose,
other than, the incredible elegance
of mathematical and cosmological coincidences.

So, the bedside work done,
the doctor goes out of the glass and steel of the hospital.

A giant sad emptiness,
overtakes the usually self-assured genius.

The blank look, in the patient's eyes
has managed to escape his sterile professional world:
Haunting him like a first-year intern.

And... then...
there is the small matter of picking
an "amusing" rosé for the garden party.

And who knows? Maybe...
the new partner's *pretty*, wife, in the medical LLC,
knows how to cook?

Inspired by these amazingly brilliant personalities (i.e. lecturers of sentient life (or lives) in the cosmos) and their sordid personal scandals.

Anglo-Saxon Sounds

It must have been a nice remark:
She was smiling at him.

He had struggled rehearsing, the previous night,
to give some fluidity to the lines.

It was akin to a steeplechase:
He could not get a smooth run.

The course was full of unpronounceable consonants:
None of the slippery ease of his parents' "kitchen" Italian.
And dependable architectural enunciation of Latin.

But read... he did.
Standing at his desk. Knees buckling.
Encouraged by the teacher's quasi-maternal nods of pride.

He vaguely remembered the clapping.
The sparkle in the green eyes of the "Irish-type" girl.

And the non-sensical repetition:
"Tomorrow and tomorrow and tomorrow..."

Newly arrived immigrant in (college) English, high school class, using the generosity in the voice and smile of the teacher, to get through what amounted to unpronounceable, verbal torture.

Teenage Trans-Substantiation

Flesh... into salvation

It is often later... much too late
that we recognize our true very personal,
intimate martyrs.
Those souls that we selfishly embrace ...
so as to not sink alone.

True heroines and heroes, worthy of the Elysian fields:
Revealed in the humble material, used and abused as pivots,
in the detritus of a back seat.

Mortified flesh at the tip of our fingers:
Somehow becoming the trans-mutated mundane, into the eternal.

Appeasement of mutual carnal hunger,
ironically attempting to feed both respective souls.

Some meaning.
From the meaningless.

––––––––––––––––––

And so, she reclined...
An icon of the Old Testament, sinuous figures from his fine arts lectures.

Food... for the next minutes.
Rich ferment for future bottomless, lyrical inspiration:
Feeling guilty for both.

Body and soul doubles:
full of passive aggressivity and resigned despair.

An intoxicating brew
of warm, pliable... fleshy substance.

And the irremediability of an angry soul.

––––––––––––––––––

Bent, remodeled and swirling visions of his past,
in whiffs of catechism,
would make her regularly reappear:

A trans-mutated, sacred host-wafer.
A redemptive lamb
that would remain such, into his present.

Miraculously untouched.
Forever sinuous and vaporous.

Overlooking an abandoned rail freight yard: 1968 Vietnamese Tet offensive, in the screaming television news. Draft letter in his pants pocket. Trying to hold down desperately to the beauty of living, in the form, the body, the presence, of a working-class girl that he will leave behind, in dead-end, working class neighborhood.

Dying Glance

Long… very long… after her departure,
he had been filling his horizons
with reconstructions of her.

Disincarnated… smoldering… *still* smoldering
pieces of moments, made of her.

Hoping… like some love-struck mad scientist…
Among poisonous, *Faustian* fumes of mercury…

Or… a deluded Pygmalion…
in a sleepy daze: at the foot of the statue:
distinguishing movements of the marble, under her veils.

Or… a sun-beaten, woman-deceived,
water-starved Légionnaire:
With mountains of grainy sand starting to invade his lungs.

All of the above… and many others
—before and after these lovers—
… will die…
with what, no other creature on earth can or will ever recreate:
Her engorged, pliable, humid lips on his.

Still fighting to avoid the void!

Still Loving Life

Sinuous wisps of curving flesh.
Hints of pulsation, in the clair-obscur of early-morning light.

Echoes of whispers:
Pronounced, in half breaths.

Glimpses of a fleshy crimson paradise:
spread over wavelets, on white cotton sheets.

Enjoying the overlap:
Between body-heat and reality.

Remnants of salty residue on upper lip,
helping to reconstruct moments.

And knowing… upon knowing …
that those instants

unfurling, once again,
into visions above the softness of the pillow,

are beyond… and will remain,
the envy of an impotent and passive universe.

Hoping to die… still loving life..

AUTHOR'S NOTES

The following is a partial listing of the author's notes, follow-ups on biographical details, cultural influences etc....as well as some unabridged version of some of my notes, giving context or temporal references etc.... [not strictly alphabetical]

Air raids: The port-city of Marseille was the target of some errant allies bombings; but the area was officially and mostly an open-city after the fall of France to Nazi control. In this book, the "Oncle Jules" episode, is a fictional adaptation [recalled by older family members] of the days of grayish boredom, followed by complete panic. Our mother, trying to go to two different grammar schools, to pick up my older brother and sister, while the early waves of bombers were arriving.

Agate: In French culture, sometimes, refers to the biggest and most prized play-marble: Hence the nickname for the greenish-blue-eyed Berber girl.

"An espresso... and some romance": The author was just told of the demise of the coffee house used as a prop for this poem: Victim, among other things of the Covid19 pandemic.

Artificial intelligence [a very personal view]: The final, most sophisticated results, of a computer-driven musical composition, no matter how beautiful, would not be so... without a human ear to compose, listen and appreciate it. A sunset is not aware of its beauty: humans are. Not unlike these events, where they have tied paint brushes to donkeys; or given brushes to monkeys, and cut up the resulting canvases: The conscious, human intent has to be there: The purpose.

Barka ("Maman Barka"): —lady from Salé—as compared to Maman Maman and Maman Malou (my sister). She would help with house and family routine. She was a major presence in the author's youth [hence the prefix, "Maman"] to whom she spoke often in *Chleuh*, a Berber language.

See "Imprinted Presence."

Very sickly, not eating and not sleeping, Barka was successful in putting me to sleep with the native tradition of wrapping children in large shawls on their backs and going about her day. She also had success in feeding me "Mesh Mesh" [apricots] and other delicious Moroccan meals, that I would call out in "Chleuh."

Barthes, Roland: mentioned in this book for his coinage of "le plaisir du texte" (la nouvelle critique), which *tries* to capture the essence, the ingredients… that extra wording… that makes *reading a particular passage pleasurable, basically, beyond any explanation:* a "je-ne-sais-quoi."For a world like mine, of poetic prose, (the sub-title of this book), it is a perfect catch-all phrase.

Excerpts from an analysis of Barthes: « Que savons-nous du texte ? ["What is text?"] La théorie, ces derniers temps, a commencé de répondre. Reste une question : que jouissons-nous du texte ? Cette question, il faut la poser, ne serait-ce que pour une raison tactique : il faut affirmer **le plaisir du texte** [author's bold type] contre les indifférences de la science et le puritanisme de l'analyse idéologique ; il faut affirmer la jouissance du texte contre l'aplatissement de la littérature à son simple agrément. Comment poser cette question? Il se trouve que le propre de la jouissance, c'est de ne pouvoir être dite. Il a donc fallu s'en remettre à une succession incoordonnée de fragments facettes, touches, bulles, phylactères d'un dessin invisible : simple mise en scène de la question, rejeton hors-science de l'analyse textuelle. »

Beauté du diable: Referring to the attraction of the Devil [Lucifer], reputedly the prettiest of the Angels: God's favorite. Here, again, it is the duality of the persona, that is of interest to the author.

Beatrice: Only mentioned once in this book, but her role as a guide for Dante, instructs my same use of the persona of "Sidi Moussa" in my work. Sidi Moussa… being the Arabic for "Lord Moses" … a presence throughout my writings.

Berbers: Indigenous people of North Africa. Berbers had extensive historical relationships with the roman Empire. Their lands and Roman-Berber cities were eventually Islamized.

Bled: Moroccan for "fields," open or empty [arid] spaces.

Madame Bovary: One of the reference texts for the evolution of the novel. A sort of emotional post-mortem of a woman in love with love, in a world and society sterilized of all sentimentality by a merciless, surgical writer's tone and style.

Camus: Albert Camus... image of secular righteousness and general ethics... should have a whole section to his name... for his central importance in all my writing. The more I read about the writer (especially the man, his personal and self-recognized weaknesses), the more I sense a doppelgänger in him: His background and his private life eerily similar. But it is that sense of "secular humanism"; the deep "moralist" in the person... although with his painful awareness of the loneliness of that afflicts humanity, that resonates in the giant figure.

Caravaggio: Although less mentioned in this book, I can't help think of his paintings, when working with any "carnality" ... "pliable flesh."

Cosmology: In this book, cosmology is a quasi-stand-in for things that allow some of us, artists and dreamers, to see (as in Plato's cave) the shadow of the divine, the finger prints of something that has evolved in time: Thus creating... 'Time itself." [see Prof Krauss]

Coupons (food): In the context of food shortages (related to me) during the German occupation. The reference to the "unmarried mother" [a real person and very loving mother for her "bastard son"] having extra coupons, implied her "sleeping" with the enemy, by the other jealous tenants.

Ex Machina: Of interest in the poem is the lack of human control.

Lawrence Krauss: I like the man. I'm using him as a straw-man of these personalities that we run into: Smart beyond belief; with a little boyish smirk, when he says... off-the-cuff... side-comments things... that send you back to research sites. Unfortunately, like too many very bright persons, his jaded interpersonal issues show us, how mankind... did evolve from the smartest apes (but ...apes, nevertheless). His "A universe from nothing" lecture, is a masterpiece that helps redeem his down-to-Earth peccadillos.

From my notes on Prof Lawrence Krauss':

" .. out of nothing… into nothing. Professor Krauss put into flowing thought what my poetry was, all that time, trying to paint. Being guided by the ultimate acceptance [not belief but scientific reality] of the bankruptcy or dead end scientific knowledge … as long as we all know that knowing ..or not knowing… that BEING OR BEING… is the same… [several universes…. with several restarts… several versions of us…] you are left with the exhilarating feeling of the "next minutes"
"The uncanny dichotomy of going to the other side
Seeing there is nothing there
And come back to yours…
And yet, still feel the humanist in you… continue." [j-y.s]"

Notes for **Flaubert's "Éducation sentimentale":** "For certain men, the stronger their desire, the less likely they are to act." Having read this synopsis on line, I decided to play God and change [in my poem] the ending and have a grandiose, carnal and especially poetic consummation between Frederic and Madame Arnoux.

Faire la queue: To wait in line, but in this poem, it is the undisciplined French attitude of "waiting their turn."

France '68: [la Belle Ferronnière] Times of incredible excitement, chaos, energy and social freedoms. In this text, it is the impact that the real life of the protagonists of the poem [one lovingly and honestly religious, a future priest]… the other lovingly and honestly non-believer… paralleling some of the movies scenarios of the time [Truffaut's "Jules et Jim"…in particular.] as well as several mentions of the U.S draft. [The Vietnam War etc…]

Grasse: the little town of Grasse, in the Alpes-Maritimes, is known for its flower-base perfume industry. My poetry refers to the various perfume of my youth from all the women around our house and my mother's office: In particular "L'heure du temps," which I reference in another poem.

Gershwin, "Rhapsody in Blue": I have to include this musical reference from my note for this book. It is about THIS particular music piece, this particular orchestra, this particular video* and angle shots…. that gave me the idea of writing a poem about the contradictions in our human natures between the **sublime and the grotesque** as Victor Hugo had put it. The vaporous and the mud. Beautiful music, from beautiful cultures, that would give rise to such a thing as Nazi Germany. And so…. as the camera zoomed around the orchestra-players, I fancied, the lead violinist having a destructive affair with the trumpet player... that everyone knew that it was their last time playing for this orchestra etc... [but truth be told... it was the stupendous talent and good looks of the pianist and the lead violinist, two feet behind him, in most of the shots]

* inspired and written as a reaction to the spectacular production of: Gershwin's "Rhapsody in Blue"
Jan 17, 2018
Royal Academy of Music
Edward Gardner conducts the Royal Academy of Music Symphony Orchestra for George Gershwin's Rhapsody in Blue with **soloist Adrian Brendle.**

Hassan Tower (Mosque) Tour Hassan: Located on the estuary between Rabat on the side of "la Kasbah des Oudaias" ... and is across from Salé [and the Kasbah of the "Chella "side (to the north). One of the most imposing minarets in the world. The structure was part of the author's youth: on a hill, on the southern bank of the [river] Oued bou Regreg. A structure, part of any of my family travel into Rabat. The Hassan Tower (Solinga family black and white photo), on page 93, twas aken late 1940's, early 1950's, with rudimentary camera and film (hence the grainy quality). This is the angle from the dining room.

The Hammurabi code of laws: A collection of 282 rules, of ancient Mesopotamia, dated to about 1754 BC , established standards for commercial and sociatal interactions and set fines and punishments to meet the requirements of justice. Hammurabi's Code was carved onto a massive, finger-shaped black stone stele (pillar) that was looted by invaders and finally rediscovered in 1901. It is currently on display in the Louvre.

Humanity vs mankind: My document/text has (hopefully) been checked for the collective neutral "humankind/humanity."

Imprinted Presence: [from extended notes] The comparison with young ducklings being imprinted with their mother's presence is perfect for a short hand description of how I had to answer loaded questions [during the oral] about my position toward the subject of my doctoral thesis. That is: That mine... did not feel as the glance of the "other" upon this landscape which, a priori felt so "normal" to me. [re: **Imprinted Presence"** (I saw it every day, of my earliest recollections of life)]. I... simply, I did not feel like an intruder in the Maghreban landscape: **It truly had the loving face of a woman in a djellaba.**

Immigration: [the other] Wide topic, covered over several other poems in previous books; but most important, is references the various episodes in the life of the author, and the changes and crises in society along the way. These two particular poems, try to keep their footing in my observations as [white] newcomer to America.

« Je t'aime... moi, non plus. »: Antithetical French movie title of the 60's early 70's. **"I love you... neither do I."** Telling statement about the times: Flexible morals and mores; in this case, open relationships. Questioning of "bourgeois" rules. Younger generations, wanting to revamp everything.

Job [Prophet]: Of interest in the poem is the idea of a religious icon such this Prophet, described as "Nihilistic."

Kesra: Flatten ball of bread: Author's vivid memories of the smiling local baker handing the still warm piece, while his mother watched the quasi ceremony. The universality of the aroma is unescapable.

La Belle Ferronnière: From the author's notes regarding that painting: "...La Belle...Ferronnière[... in spite of a fuzzy artistic provenance and biographical details of the real person portraited... what counted for the author is the realism of this viewer, who was first introduced to her as a young man... back to France, since leaving it for America as a young teenager. *She* was in a discreet space among "others" in the Louvre. The Mona Lisa [la Joconde], gloriously alone on her wall [circa 1970] ... he never forgot her glance [the one of "la Ferronnière" and not of the Mona Lisa] ... did not care about her suspect pedigree.... He could not forget her big eyes... full of Mediterranean heat... like the waitress at his university hangout who would invade his life...." [from author's notebook].

LeClézio, Jean-Marie Gustave: Twentieth century lyrical writer of impeccable, stylistic elegance of his landscapes. My reading of his *Désert*, was like finding my lost intellectual brother. LeClézio had written exactly what I was inadequate to do: so, I included him in one of my chapter of my doctoral thesis. His description of the young Maghreban girl... **Lalla**, returning pregnant from Paris, to give birth, alone, on the desert floor: "...

her thighs opened…" to the starry night of the desert, is nothing short of biblical.

Legrand, Michel: French composer and lyricist. One his most iconic work is "**les Moulins de mon coeur**," "The Windmills of my mind." [not sure of the reason for the change form the French "heart"] [the French lyrics that start with the preposition [or adverb] "Comme…" are clearly built like a very long [and beautiful] simile.

Les Poètes maudits: [**the Damned *(Lost)* Poets:** Early, to middle nineteenth century French poets: such as Baudelaire, Verlaine. Rimbaud, Musset, Vigny… . they manipulated with artistry, dissipated mores and very modern, remorseful self-reflection.

Like "Ducklings": Short-hand term for author to delve into the treacherous topic of the presence of the "colon" [the colonialist] and his [inbred] childhood attachment to the land. [see Camus]

Lyrical prose: My tool against the dehumanizing effects of artificial intelligence: In particular on the lyricism of language. [the *purposeful lyricism*]. The author was inspired to use this hybrid tone, in particular, by Camus' and LeClézio's style and their analytical adaptation to make **impeccable thinking… beautiful.**

In "Untold Years into the Future," I used this type of lyricism as the last bastion of *resistance* **of the separation, between human and machine** derived poetry: With the hopes that there might be a happy ending for in a human, *organic, carnal…* advantage.

The following are French and English lyrics of the poetic intent that will separate [for a little while longer?] human-created lyricism as compared to code-generated, artificial intelligence composition, [see "Untold Years into the Future"]:

Windmills of Your Mind [words and music Michel Legrand]

Round like a circle in a spiral, like a wheel within a wheel
Never ending or beginning on an ever spinning reel
Like a snowball down a mountain, or a carnival balloon
Like a carousel that's turning running rings around the moon

Like a clock whose hands are sweeping past the minutes of its face
And the world is like an apple whirling silently in space
Like the circles that you find in the windmills of your mind!

Songwriters: Marilyn Bergman / Michel Legrand / Alan Bergman
"Windmills of Your Mind" lyrics © Sony/ATV Music Publishing LLC, BMG
Rights Management
Les moulins de mon cœur
By Michel Legrand, Natalie Dessay

Comme une pierre que l'on jette dans l'eau vive d'un ruisseau
Et qui laisse derrière elle des milliers de ronds dans l'eau
Comme un manège de lune avec ses chevaux d'étoiles
Comme un anneau de Saturne, un ballon de carnaval
Comme le chemin de ronde que font sans cesse les heures
Le voyage autour du monde d'un tournesol dans sa fleur
Tu fais tourner de ton nom tous les moulins de mon cœur

The preceding French and English versions of that incomparable tour
de force by Michel Legrand' long simile ["comme"/ "like"], which would
not "amuse" machines... is all about... **human lyricism.** It is a concrete
example for my "credo" (my secular belief... therefore, no capitalization)
that lyricism will be... for **human thought**, what we call... **human
emotions**...our last line of defense against the pernicious, **frigid efficiency,
of artificial intelligence**, that will blur what it is "to be human...or feel
human emotions." [in the poem, I was thinking: "What would Captain Kirk,
of the Enterprise, do" to prove his superiority over machines? [assuming,
that French is still taught, that far in the future, in schools and that Kirk
would be bi-lingual]

Maghreb: [the "solar" world, full of the beauty and *contradictory currents* of
recent history The *setting sun* [literally] in Arabic. Collective name of people,
civilizations, cultures, cities and ruins [in particular today's Morocco,
Tunisia, Algeria]. In this book [and others] there are references of the role
of these places and cross-cultural contacts, that Algeria and Morocco, have
played in the author's life. As well as, being the setting for major figures and
places for some poems: "The plague" [**"La peste"**], "Les noces," by Camus.
And the author's doctoral thesis: an analysis of the landscape of North
Africa on several French writers.

Madonna: Of interest [like Marie Antoinette] in this book, for her unabashed pride in her sexuality and one of the first to be successful and apparently happy [in Madonna's case] in her flaunting endeavor. [less so for

Malle, Louis: And his autobiographical movie, "Au revoir les enfants." The movie's title are the last words of the caring, gentle priest, as he is taken to his death, by the Germans. It encapsulates the grandiose mastery of details of Louis Malle.
Marie Antoinette, who was... maligned and guillotined]

Marquis: "Le Marquis de Sade," is the reference in the context of this book: I use this controversial figure of history as a metric of thinkers who were instrumental in breaking western thinking away from mindless religiosity. As it is often the case in these attempts, by unbridled (juvenile) passion.

Mona Lisa: la Joconde: Of interest in this book, in her role in the author seeing La Ferronnière [attributed to de Vinci] a few feet away at the Louvre of the 1970's. Though the ... La Ferronnière, is a lesser painting: Of dubious provenance, the author was shaken in looking at the "glance" of La Ferronnière: A doppelgänger of someone he knew. In his notes, the author entered: "In spite of the fuzzy provenance and the disagreements about the real person behind it... what counts, is the realism that the viewer sees in it]. The author's notes entered: "I was first introduced to her as a young man... in a discreet space among "others... the Mona Lisa gloriously alone on her wall [circa 1970] I never forgot her glance... did not care about her suspect pedigree.... I could not forget her... her big eyes... full of Mediterranean heat... like the waitress at my university hangout... the one who would invade my life with *that kiss.*

(Madame) Bovary: one of the greatest realistic analysis of emotions and society by an author who was a romantic at heart, but wrote with a merciless, critical eye.

Minotaur: I like the idea that in this figure of mythology we have a child of a woman [Pasiphae] and a bull. Like Prometheus and Sisyphus, I like their **quasi-human passions and complexity.** they seem more complex [yes... human] figures.

Modelé: The rendition, in painting and sculpting, of the corporal form under clothing.

"Newly off the Boat": from the author's notes: "The implied racial topic of the poem and its life-long consequences, are encapsulated in the French saying: "Au pays des aveugles, les borgnes sont les rois." (In the land of the blinds… the one-eyed seeing persons are kings."). This came to mind after the author's observation of his natural, "blending-in status," as a white person, upon his walking off the vessel from France, in the streets of a New York of the 1950's.[Nota bene: the change from being sighted to having only one nose.] the preceding were the original marginal comments on the poem."

Nihilism: Of interest for the author for its imposition on mankind to formulate its own ethics. In this book, it is the ultimate ethical integrity for someone like a Docteur Rieux (a nihilist) to fight a losing battle against the plague: Expecting no divine intervention or reward.

Noces: One of the earliest writings by a young Albert Camus. The little book [really a notebook] was a revelation to a generation of university students. [including this author]. It is a splendid reflection on mankind and the senses.

Oswiecim: In Polish. Auschwitz in German.

Occupation: German occupation of France and the numerous lessons in human kindness and betrayals from unexpected sources. Such as church-attending adults, not sharing food with needy, co-tenant, families. (see "A Virtuous Soul").

"The Omega man": The interest in this book, for this "sci-fi" movie with Charlton Heston, is again the idea of these **pseudo "mythological" figures** of mankind/mortals, against the gods/ nature/the cosmos. Also, the not too distant or improbable, post global-pandemic story of a world of survival.

Phaedra: Of interest in this book, as one of the most tragic figure of a woman's passion. Iconic figure destroyed by her [rebellious] love for her step son. (source of many tragedies: among which Phèdre by Pierre Racine.)

Planet of the apes: Post dystopian, post-apocalyptic, war story of the taking-over of the planet, by apes: And of interest, for this book, the intersection and interaction between pro-human apes… etc. Rebellion against the new order is never quieted.

Plato: First the allegory of the Cave, which the author finds intriguing because it deal with a **topic of constant interest to the author: Reality.** [re: Solinga, *Created Realities*]. Without going into the details, which can be found in references, it seems to the author and to more scientists, that *what we thought… that we thought…* was unarguably a certain, stable, continuing thing… which, after all… may… or may not, have been the case. We are finding out that things [space and time: i.e. many universes and several Big Bangs] are bigger and more numerous, than we thought. While the small, is getting smaller, notwithstanding Democritus and his "Atom."

Plato2: Of interest in this book, is the myth of the cave, where the philosopher dealt with mankind dealing with **various states and forms of reality.** (re. cosmology)

Place Saint-Michel: Quartier Latin, Paris on the way to l'île de la Cité, and the setting of numerous, pivotal poems by the author.

Poetry/Poetic Prose/Lyrical Prose: Charles Baudelaire very purposefully worked with the musicality of words. To that end, he coined "Vers en prose" ["Poetic verses in prose style"] etc. But it is the intersection of **beautiful sounds and incisive thought** that Camus and LeClezio have matched so well.

Prometheus: In this book, it is the "**rebellious Titan**" aspect that is so awe-inspiring in this figure: a subordinate [just a Titan] who challenges the gods; stealing their "fire": Bringing it to mortals/mankind, thus risking an unending, divine-instigated torture.

Prometheus Carrying Fire: Had been a possible cover for book: Jan Cossiers (1600-1671) Prado Museum. The author thought it to be "too muscular." Therefore, opted, instead, for the Rockefeller Center statue: More in the image of the of the **duality** [his slander built] of the Titan.

Place de Clichy: mentioned by name or not, this Place in Paris is mentally, emotionally perceived by the author in describing the "feel" of the city. It encapsulates the author's romantic world of Paris and is therefore a template for the romanticism, of the "miniscule bedroom" scenes, of his work. Not far from Pigalle, la Place Blanche: its marginal life: contrasted by le Sacré Coeur, on its hill.

Rabat mosque: this majestic mosque on a hilltop overlooking the Oued bou Regreg, is indelibly imprinted on the author's mind: It is one of his first earliest memory of anything. Could it be also true for mankind as it is for ducklings, that one sees the face of his "mother" in the first glance? The mosque was literally across from the living room window from Salé on the northern side. La Tour Hassan [Rabat. Maroc] is one of the of the most imposing view in the country.

Reality [cosmos]: Plays a huge role in the author's work. (see "Created Realities") But in this book, it is the cutting-edge, sciences of what we understand as "reality." As of the writing, one of the theories of the so called empty space between galaxies etc… may not be empty at all…but instead, full of some primordial "gunk-cloud."

Reality [literary]: the author's interplay between reality and fiction can better be exemplified in specific poems. In "Saint Sulpice Seminary," for instance, there are two sources for the "priest" [or future priest], of the poem. One, American-Francophile; the other, Spanish, in the middle of the chaos of a "dying" Generalissimo Franco. Befriended during a visit of the Prado: we had an instantaneous relationship, when I asked him [in civilian clothing], where the Bosch exhibit was. He whispered that the Guardia civil didn't like to advertise the location: And then proceeded to shepherd me around [whispering all the time].

Another example of my use and **manipulation of Reality** throughout my work is my source, lyrical [especially love-themed] poems. This is where [as I told a fellow writer who had a couple of irritated ex-wives] Proust's pastiche is an excellent tool: The more opaque the better. My material can be very real; but untraceable. It helps my "sleep of the justs."

Reality 2: As seen through Plato's Myth of the cave: the intelligible [the forms] are reality. Plato may also be inviting us to the mysticism of "knowing."

Rif: Arid, difficult mountainous area at the northeastern tip off Morocco. Perfect setting for recurring pockets of political and social rebellions.

Rum, Rûmi: Generally speaking, this term refers to "roman" or from Rome: Referring to descendants of Roman soldiers in North Africa. The whole of the northern African continent had been "Romanized": particularly what is today's Tunisia.. The Berber population was therefore affected. Although the "Rum" were associated with Byzantium, the Roman culture and language (as well as their legions) created an intermingling with the population: Thus the reference in this text to "eyes" of the Berber girl as possibly having the ancestry of a Northern European legionnaire.

Sagan, Carl: unusual combination of a great scientific mind, but a lyrical view of mankind's place in the cosmos. His commentary on Voyager 1's pictures, of our miniscule planet in the vastness of a black universe tells it all.

Sisyphus: [rebellious personae, like Prometheus] Titan who challenges the gods and is punished by having to endlessly push a bolder up a hill, to only have it roll back down.

Soylent Green: Dystopian world of **over-population**: The name is the source of food [wafers, maybe made of... cadavers? for the masses.

Space: Might not be what we think it is: The extremely small might represent the same problem: There seems to be no easy answer to what we thought had been solved by the Greek Democritus [in ~450 B.C. , i.e. the atom] is not that simple: Scientists keep finding smaller and smaller units to what exists

Secular humanism: Term that encompasses the various beliefs and ethical issues of humanity without the overarching belief or interaction in God.

Sentimental education: "Éducation sentimentale" 19th century novel by Gustave Flaubert, considered one of the finest examples the **realism of human emotions.**

The Telagh: Town in the commune of Sidi Bel Abbès [birth place of the author], in north-western Algeria.

Truffaut, François: director of **nouvelle vague** movies. Adapted the Hollywood technique of shooting "night scenes" [Day for night] with filters [Nuit américaine].

The Rebel "L'Homme Révolté": In this book it is especially the observation made by Camus to differentiate **rebellion from révolution**. One the result of an individual against his oppressor... the other one of a collective act of a people comes to mind... the statement... the credo, that echoes Descartes' "cogito ... ergo sum.": "I think thererore I am.." Which has been changed to: **"I rebel... therefore... we are..."**.

Tipasa: Roman ruins in coastal North African roman province (now Algeria).

Trans-substantiation: The concept of and ritual in the Christian church of transforming bread into the body of Christ. In the poem, it is purposefully strong and borderline blasphemous, to compare the activity in the back of that car... to the transformation (or the use) of that girl's [mortified] flesh for such a selfish purpose.

From notes for book: Reflections on **post world war two European** theater, with its remnants of 'architectural bones' of exquisite beauty, artistic achievements (particularly music) and the unimaginable **horrors and contradictions in our humanity that somehow co-exist** in all of us. [topic and theme for a poem: A spectacular recording of some musical suite in a cathedral that had seen World War Two atrocities.]

Zeus [the god of gods]: Of interest to the author, since Zeus would be the **ultimate prosecutor of infractions and rebellions.** Rebellion, however, is by definition, an individual act. Thus very precious to Camus as his "L'Homme révolté"... "The Rebel," shows. Hence the following paraphrase about his book/essay... "I rebel... therefore, we exist." Of similar interest is the figure of Prometheus who sacrifices himself, through his rebellious act, and will suffer for eternity for the betterment of mortals. By his actions, a Titan... worthy of being one of us mortals.

INDEX

Titles in bold and first lines in italics.

About the Author

Jean-Yves Solinga

Jean-Yves' family comes from Provence. He was born in Algeria, and lived thereafter between the south of France and Morocco in what he describes as an idyllic youth. Upon settling in America with his family, at the age of 15, he had already been writing poetry: being first published, in English, in *A Letter Among Friends* along with Jon Norman of New London, CT. After serving in the U.S. Army, he began a successful career in teaching, translating and lecturing. Jean-Yves holds a doctorate in French on the representation of the Maghreban [North African] landscape found in the texts by Pierre Loti, André Gide, Albert Camus, and Jean-Marie Le Clézio.

He has published, to date, ten books of poetry: *Clair-Obscur of the Soul* (2008), *Clair-obscur de l'âme* [in French] (2008), *In the Shade of a Flower* (2009), *Landscape of Envies* (2010), *Words Made of Silk* (2011), *Impressions of Reality* (2013), *Artist in a Pixelated World* (2014), *Asymptotes at the Limit of Passion* (2015), *Created Realities* (2017), and *Paris: Genesis of a Muse (2019)*. [unpublished: Sidi Moussa: la jeunesse se perd... mais pas la passion. Poèmes en marge de Sidi Moussa. Sidi Moussa: poems from the Labrador.]. This book will make eleven books in twelve years.

Jean-Yves's poetry continues to use an infrastructure of poetic or lyrical prose. He aims for a linguistic landscape that lives between the inevitability of hard reality and the aspirating appeal of vaporous passion: Exploring the contrasting worlds of the euphoria of sensual happiness and the inevitability of its demise.

Many of his poems have a personal, as well as societal breath. It is often a singularly unique view of mankind's reflection through the prism of the lyrical language with, at times an impressionistic poetry, tackling many hard realities of history and society.

Jean-Yves Solinga is a poet of immense ability and range whose lyricism is truly remarkable. It contains many breathtakingly beautiful and sophisticated poems that reach out to the very limits of the human condition where true art exists. Many facets of his work continue to find inspiration and perspective in his cultural duality.

www.ingramcontent.com/pod-product-compliance
Lightning Source LLC
Chambersburg PA
CBHW080735250626

47170CB00010B/2832